D1321213

St Elizabeth's Children's Hospital

Mills & Boon® Medical™ Romance
welcomes you to
St Elizabeth's Children's Hospital…

Amongst the warmth and heartache,
the laughter and tears, these
medical professionals, devoted to their
young patients, find love and true happiness
where they least expect it…

So come on in and meet them for yourselves!

Look out for more stories set at St Elizabeth's
this month from
Mills & Boon® Medical™ Romance

Caroline Anderson has the mind of a butterfly. She's been a nurse, a secretary, a teacher, run her own soft-furnishing business, and now she's settled on writing. She says, 'I was looking for that elusive something. I finally realised it was variety, and now I have it in abundance. Every book brings new horizons and new friends, and in between books I have learned to be a juggler. My teacher husband John and I have two beautiful and talented daughters, Sarah and Hannah, umpteen pets, and several acres of Suffolk that nature tries to reclaim every time we turn our backs!' Caroline also writes for the Mills & Boon® Romance series.

Recent titles by the same author:

Medical™ Romance

THE VALTIERI MARRIAGE DEAL
A MUMMY FOR CHRISTMAS
THEIR MIRACLE BABY*
CHRISTMAS EVE BABY*

Mills & Boon® Romance

TWO LITTLE MIRACLES
THE SINGLE MUM AND THE TYCOON
HIS PREGNANT HOUSEKEEPER

Brides of Penhally Bay

ANGEL'S CHRISTMAS

BY
CAROLINE ANDERSON

First published in Great Britain 2000
This edition 2010
Harlequin Mills & Boon Limited,
Eton House, 18-24 Paradise Road, Richmond, Surrey TW9 1SR

© Caroline Anderson 2000

ISBN: 978 0 263 21483 3

Harlequin Mills & Boon policy is to use papers that are natural,
renewable and recyclable products and made from wood grown in
sustainable forests. The logging and manufacturing process conform
to the legal environmental regulations of the country of origin.

Printed and bound in Great Britain
by CPI Antony Rowe, Chippenham, Wiltshire

ANGEL'S CHRISTMAS

PROLOGUE

'MARIA, we have to talk about this—'

'No!' Her eyes were wide, wild with anger and something else—something that could have been a feverish excitement. 'I don't want to talk any more! We talk and talk—all the time we talk, but there's nothing to talk about! I don't want to live with you— I don't want to live in England. I want to be here, with my family!'

She snatched up her bag and seized Angel by the arm, dragging her towards his borrowed car. 'I tell you this over and over, but you don't listen! Well, now you listen! It's over, Robert. Angelique and I live here now, in Oporto, with Carlos—'

'Carlos?' He was stunned. 'You're living with *Carlos*?'

She folded her arms and gave him an arch look. 'Oh, you didn't know about Carlos? I thought you knew everything, Robert—I thought you were so damn clever! Well, you're not! You're not clever at all.'

He felt sick. She couldn't take his Angel! Poor baby, she'd hate it here, surrounded by strangers, without him to turn to. How could she do this to her? To all of them?

'Maria, please, we have to talk about this—'

'Here you go again! Talk, talk, talk! No, Robert. It's over. Angelique is coming with me.'

'But what about me? She loves me—'

'What *about* you? She loves me, too—and I'm her mother!'

'I'm her father!'

A brow arched. 'Are you?' She turned to Angel, standing wide-eyed between them, her face anxious. 'Get in the car,' she ordered.

Robert felt for the car keys in his pocket and sighed with relief. Without the keys she couldn't go anywhere. 'Angel, come here,' he said softly.

'No! Angel, remember—' The child looked at her mother, who broke into hurried Portuguese. Robert didn't understand everything that she was saying, but apparently Angel did, and her face crumpled.

She went woodenly to the car—the big, open-topped sports model he'd borrowed that morning from Carlos—and climbed into the front passenger seat. Robert didn't bother to move. Maria would find out soon enough that the keys weren't in it. Then all hell would break loose, of course.

Maria slid behind the wheel, and from her bag she produced a jangling keyring and slid a key into the ignition. The horror must have shown on his face, because she threw back her head and laughed. 'Oh, yes, Robert—Carlos and I share everything—even his car. So of course, I too have the keys! I'll see you in hell!'

And before he could reach her, she twisted the key, gunned the engine and shot off down the drive, skidding round the first hairpin bend on her way down to the road, her laughter echoing in the air behind her. He ran to the low parapet wall, watching in despair as his wife drove away with his daughter—his beloved, precious daughter, the only thing in their tragically poisonous relationship that was worth having.

It had taken three weeks and some serious talking to get her address out of her family, and then oddly enough it had been Carlos who had yielded, and even lent him the car to find her. Carlos who, by all accounts, was her lover. And now she was running from him in that car, and he had no way of following her and no idea how he'd find her again.

He stared helplessly as the car skidded and fishtailed down the drive to the mountain road below—sliding onto it in the path of an oncoming lorry. The driver leant on his horn, and the car swerved round it and straightened.

'Dear God,' he muttered in disbelief. 'She's going to kill them both if she goes on like that!' Sick horror rose up to choke him, and his fingers gripped the wall so hard his nails tore.

For a moment he thought it would be all right, that the car would hold the road, but then suddenly it lost traction, the back flying out and smacking into the low wall at the side of the steep ravine. For a second it hovered, teetering on the brink, then as if in slow motion the car began to slide through the shattered wall, then rolled, end over end, down into the ravine, crashing through the undergrowth with a hideous tearing sound that made his blood run cold.

There was a stunned silence for a second, when even the birds seemed to hold their breath, and then a dull 'whump!', and a huge ball of flame rose up out of the ravine, raining debris.

'Angel?' he whispered. 'Oh, God. Oh, no—Angel, no—!'

Then he started to run...

CHAPTER ONE

'I'LL come back as soon as I can, sweetheart—I promise.'

Angel's damp, dark eyes stared up at him in a silent plea. 'I don't want you to go,' she whispered, and his heart contracted.

'Darling, it's not for long. I just need to go and see Daniel and put my things in his flat, then I'll be back. Just an hour—no more.'

'The last time you said that you were *ages*,' she said accusingly, and guilt clawed at him for the thousandth time.

'I know, and I'm sorry. I couldn't help it. This time I really will be quick. I promise.'

'You will come back?'

He laid a hand over hers, gripping his fingers tightly, and nodded. 'Of course I'll come back. Wild horses wouldn't keep me away.'

Her little hand released him. 'OK,' she said mournfully. 'Just don't forget about me.'

'Angel, I never forget about you. Not for a minute,' he assured her with considerable truth. He stood up and bent over her, kissing her softly on her satin-smooth cheek, and then left, quickly, before she could see the tears gathering in his eyes.

'OK?' a nurse said brightly, and he nodded, pulling himself together.

'I have to go and drop my things off with a

friend—Dr Burr? I'm going to be staying with him. I'll be back as soon as I can.'

'You can stay here—I'm sure we can find you somewhere if it would help.'

He shook his head. 'I'll be working in the hospital from Friday, so I'll need my sleep—anyway, she's used to it. She seems to have spent most of the past eighteen months in hospital. Don't worry, I'll be here as much as I can.'

The nurse smiled. 'All right. I'll make sure she's nice and busy so she hardly knows you've gone.'

'Thanks.'

He headed down the ward away from his daughter, turning at the door to wave, but already she was engrossed in conversation with the nurse. In truth it was him and not her that found the thought of her forthcoming surgery so hard. She had been strangely insistent about it.

He was worried about her, unable to put his finger on what was wrong but equally unable to bring back the sparkle into her life. Perhaps this operation would do it, but he had his doubts.

There was just something different about her dealings with him now, something that had shifted since the accident, as if the footings holding up the very structure of their relationship had fractured invisibly.

Damn Maria, he thought, and then stopped himself. She'd been damned enough. She'd paid with her life.

And left their daughter with a legacy of pain and disfigurement that nothing could completely take away...

Robert pulled up outside the tall, converted Victorian house where Daniel lived, and cut the engine.

Amazingly there was unrestricted parking, and, even more amazingly, a space right outside. He would lay odds it was the last time it would happen to him.

Still, Daniel had said there was some parking available—perhaps it was round the back. He locked the car, pocketed the keys and walked up the dimly lit path, just as a young woman with windswept brown hair and hands full of shopping bags struggled up to the front door.

She stepped inside the circle of light that spread out from the entrance just as she looked up at him, and for a moment it seemed to Robert as if the light were coming from within her.

Absurd.

She gave him a friendly smile, and the light seemed paradoxically brighter. 'Hi,' she said. 'I don't suppose you could open the door for me, could you? My keys are somewhere in my coat pocket and if I put this lot down now I'll never pick them up again!'

He found himself smiling back without thinking, drawn in by the warmth in her green-gold eyes and the kindness of her face.

She looks like a mother, he thought—serene and comforting. Lucky kids, I bet she's wonderful. He had another pang of guilt and grief for his motherless child and dragged himself back to here and now. 'Um—I don't have any keys. I was just going to ring the bell.'

'Oh—well, to save you doing that, why don't you find my keys and let us both in? It's freezing out here.'

'I might be an axe-murderer,' he pointed out, and she laughed, a warm, soft chuckle that tickled his senses.

'I don't think so. You haven't got the eyes for it.'
She lifted her arm up to give him access to her pocket,
and he found his hand snuggled in there next to the
warmth of her body. Heat shot through him, and he
gave an almost silent grunt of irritation at himself. It
was just a pocket, for goodness' sake! A baggy old
coat pocket full of sweet wrappers and used bus tickets—nothing that ought to turn him on! What a sad,
sick old man he was turning into—

His fingers found the keys and latched onto them
with almost religious fervour. 'Here,' he said, sighing
with relief, and drew them out. 'Which key?'

'The one with the red tag. That's it. Thanks.' The
door swung open, and she went inside and pushed in
the light switch with her shoulder, one of those timed
ones that turned off by themselves after a couple of
minutes, and then flashed him that radiant smile
again.

'You couldn't open the flat as well, could you? My
fingers have gone dead with the weight of the shopping and when I put it down the circulation's going
to come back, and I'm probably going to scream.' She
nodded at a door, setting her glossy hair bouncing and
shimmering in the stark light of the hall. 'It's this one.
Green tag this time.'

He opened the door for her, pushing it so that she
could go in, and she crossed the threshold and
dumped her shopping, hugging her fingers under her
arms. 'Ouch,' she said with a smile, and he felt his
heart warm. She really was a love—so nice and un-
affected.

He withdrew the keys and handed them to her as
she flicked on the light, and she took them, in red-
and-white striped fingers, and smiled again. 'Thanks.'

'My pleasure.'

She started to close the door, and he held up his hand to stop her, a thought occurring to him.

'Before you go—I don't suppose you know which flat's Daniel Burr's, do you?' he asked.

The door was whipped wide open again, and her green-gold eyes searched his face with undisguised curiosity. 'Upstairs—right at the top. Are you Robert Oliver?'

He nodded, wondering how she knew, then working it out. 'Yes—and you must be Maddie, then?'

She grinned, seeming pleased that he knew of her. 'That's right. I expect he's warned you about me. I'd shake hands but they hurt too much. Go on up and see him—he should be there. He left early today, with Annie—sorry, Sarian. She was attacked at work—'

'Attacked?' he echoed, sickened at yet another example of the vulnerability of hospital staff. 'Is she all right?'

'I think so,' Maddie reassured him. 'It was nothing serious, she was frightened more than anything, but Dan's such a worrywart over her. He wanted to make sure she was OK. I'm sure they'll be in. If not, come and kill time here. I'll put the kettle on—the door's always open.'

'Thanks.' He found himself smiling again, something that didn't happen too often these days, and, pushing the next light switch, he ran upstairs, past three other doors and on up another flight to a single door at the top. He knocked, the sound echoing sharply in the empty stairwell, and after a little while the door was opened a few inches and Daniel appeared in the gap, his hair rumpled, his eyes glazed with sleep.

They widened momentarily, then closed, and he sagged against the doorpost. 'Rob—oh, hell, I'm sorry. I forgot you were coming.' Daniel's hand scrubbed over his face and he looked up again, peering past Robert into the hallway. 'Is Angel with you?'

Robert shook his head, taking rapid inventory of his friend's disarray and the interesting colour working its way up his neck. He hadn't realised his friend's relationship with this Sarian was so far advanced. Maybe it hadn't been when they had last spoken. 'No, she's at the hospital. Is it inconvenient, Easy?' he said quietly. 'I can always come back later.'

Daniel laughed, sounding awkward and uncomfortable. He ran a hand through his tousled hair and grinned. 'Um—sort of. We were asleep. We had a bit of a shock—Sarian was attacked.'

'I gather. Is she all right?'

'Yeah, fine. Look, I'm sorry about this. Can you give us a minute?'

'Sure. I'll go and take Maddie up on her offer. She was putting the kettle on in case you were out.'

'You've met?'

'I helped her open the door just now—she had loads of shopping. We introduced ourselves—that was how I knew about Sarian. I'm sure she won't mind if I go and pester her.'

Daniel nodded distractedly. 'Just let us throw something on and we'll be down. We've got something to tell you both anyway.'

Robert nodded slowly, wondering what the something was and fairly certain he could guess. 'Sure. I'll go and introduce myself properly.'

He turned on his heel and ran downstairs, deep in thought. So Daniel had finally fallen for someone.

Well, about time. He stifled the pang of jealousy, and thought instead about Maddie and her bright smile that banished the shadows in the hallway and made something inside him come alive again. Lifting his hand, he knocked on Maddie's door and waited impatiently for her to answer it.

The knock, even though she was half expecting it, made Maddie jump. She'd been pottering in the kitchen and had just finished putting her shopping away, her mind replaying what she'd heard of Robert Oliver and what now she'd now seen, trying to mesh the two. She'd rather had the impression from Daniel that he was a bit of a lad, but he seemed quiet and thoughtful and very conservative.

Maybe he'd just grown up in the years since he and Daniel had lived together as students. He was certainly all grown up now, she thought, remembering those piercing blue-grey eyes and the firm, chiselled line of his lips. There was no trace left in him of a wild youth—he'd been all man, every last inch.

A man with the weight of the world on his shoulders, by the look in his eyes. She wondered how long it was since he'd laughed. Really laughed, till his sides ached.

Ages. Years, probably.

She started to tidy the sitting room, but at the knock she abandoned that as a hopeless task and opened the door. Robert was standing there, looking a little uncomfortable.

'Is he out?' she said sympathetically, welcoming him in. 'Never mind, the kettle's boiled.'

'Actually, he's in. They both are. He...asked me

to wait down here with you. They're coming down in a minute. They were asleep.'

Comprehension dawned, and Maddie laughed awkwardly. 'Oh. Right. Well, we'd better make that tea, then. You might as well get to know me as we're going to be working together. I'm Maddie Brooks, Junior A and E Sister, as I'm sure Daniel's told you. It's nice to meet you, I've heard a lot about you.'

She held out her hand, finally free of pins and needles, and felt it engulfed in a warm, hard hand that made her feel both safe and very, very threatened all at once.

'Robert Oliver—shortly to be your new specialist registrar—but you knew that, too.' His mouth kicked up in a smile. 'And I've heard a lot about you, too. You've been a good friend to Daniel.'

Maddie wrinkled her nose. 'I've tried. He doesn't always make it easy.'

'No.'

'Um—' She swallowed, the feel of his hand distracting her so that the connection between her brain and her mouth felt severed. She tried again. 'Tea?' she said, and he nodded, letting her go as if he'd suddenly realised he was still holding her hand and couldn't quite work out why.

'Please.' He shrugged out of his coat and looked around. 'Can I put this somewhere?'

'Of course—I'm sorry, I'm forgetting myself,' Maddie said hastily, and hung it on the back of the door. 'Come into the kitchen. Sarian's left the sitting room in a mess and I daren't touch her things. Still, Daniel will sort her out, he's even more of a neat freak than I am.'

She realised she was gabbling, and shut up, leading

him through to the kitchen. She was suddenly absurdly aware of the mug on the draining-board, the bag of rice still waiting to be tipped into the container—and the list on the fridge door under the frog magnet that said, 'New bra' in big letters at the top.

She opened the fridge and took out the milk, surreptitiously moving the frog so it covered up the word 'bra'. Not that it mattered, but she just suddenly felt self-conscious.

Pointless, really. Robert was miles away, standing at the window staring out at the bleak and barren garden—at least, what little was visible with the spill of light from the window. Conscious of the fact that the garden looked awful, and even more conscious of the yawning silence, she rushed to fill it.

'It's quite pretty in the summer, we put tubs out with geraniums and things. Daniel spends a lot of time down here—well, at least, he did,' she corrected, feeling a sudden pang of dismay. She'd enjoyed his friendship, and knew that, now Annie was part of his life, things were going to change.

She'd miss him, but only in the most platonic way, and at least she saw Annie more now than she had before.

'He said they had something to tell us,' Robert murmured, and her head flew up, her curiosity thoroughly aroused.

'Really? Like what?'

Robert shrugged. 'I don't know. An announcement, perhaps?'

Maddie searched his eyes, looking for clues, but he was either a very good poker player or he didn't know any more than he was telling. 'I wonder,' she said thoughtfully. 'It would be fantastic if it's what I think.

I love them both dearly, and if any two people deserve to be happy, it's them.'

'I never thought he would ever settle down—he's always been so casual with women, so untouched by them,' he added thoughtfully.

He wasn't untouched by Sarian, Maddie could have said, or casual with or about her, but she wasn't going to tell Robert that. It wasn't her place to talk about them, but she agreed silently. He'd never seemed to take any woman seriously, until recently. Until Annie. She poured water on the tea bags and chewed her lip thoughtfully, thinking over the events of the last few days, of Annie's head-in-the-clouds happiness when she'd appeared the other morning after spending the night with Daniel.

'I wouldn't be surprised if they were serious,' she told him, forgetting that she hadn't meant to comment. 'Annie's never been like this before either.'

'Annie?' Robert asked, turning towards her and spearing her with those strangely changeable blue-grey eyes. 'I thought her name was Sarian.'

Maddie smiled and waved her hand. 'Oh, whatever. She *is* Sarian, but she never used to call herself that. She thought her grandmother's name was a bit strange, and called herself Annie. All part of not drawing attention to herself. I can't get used to calling her Sarian, but everybody else does now. It can be a bit confusing.'

'It's like Daniel,' he agreed. 'I've always called him Easy—his middle name's Ezekiel, and it started as a joke and sort of stuck while we were training. I still say it occasionally and people think I'm mad.'

She threw him a smile. 'You and me both, then. We can be mad together.' She poured out a mug of tea and handed it to him. 'Here—we'd better drink this while we've got the chance. They'll be down in a minute.'

She hooked out a chair from the kitchen table and sank gratefully into it, offering him the other one, but he shook his head. 'I've been sitting all day—driving here, sitting with my daughter while they admitted her and checked her over, waiting for the consultant—you know the sort of thing. She's having plastic surgery tomorrow.'

'I know—Daniel said something—sorting out the aftermath of a car accident? I hope you don't mind him telling me.'

'Of course not. Gareth Davies is going to try and sort out the scarring on her face. It was repaired at the time of the accident, but saving her life and her leg was the priority. It's a mess, but Davies tells me it's possible to sort it out. I didn't want her to have it done—she's suffered enough, but she insisted.'

'How is she about it now?' Maddie asked, her heart going out to the little scrap facing such an ordeal.

He shrugged, his wide shoulders lifting slowly as if he had the weight of the world on them. 'She's gutsy, but she's scared. I'd be scared, facing that all over again, but she's utterly determined to have it done.'

'You must be tired,' she said softly, and he dropped his head against the cool glass and sighed.

'Yes,' he agreed, and she had a feeling he was talking about more than today, that it wasn't just the journey to the hospital, but the road of life itself that made him tired.

He looked old for a moment, much older than Daniel, although they were both the same age, thirty-two or thereabouts. His dark hair was touched with silver at the sides, and she wondered what the last eighteen months had done to him. It must have been hell. She had a sudden urge to hug him, to tell him that it was all right, everything would be OK, he didn't need to worry any more—but she couldn't.

It wasn't in her power to take away whatever it was that put that look in his eyes—and anyway, it wasn't her business. Annie had told her very recently to butt out and mind her own business and stop interfering.

She swallowed the little pang of hurt that memory brought, and remembered the lesson. Leave him alone, she told herself. You know he's got problems. Just keep out of it.

And then he turned, looking at her with those fathoms-deep blue-grey eyes, and she knew she couldn't keep out of it. For some unaccountable reason she already cared about him, and her damn fool interfering streak was suddenly a mile wide, and growing by the second.

Robert needed help—needed someone to listen, to talk to, to tell his problems to in the middle of the night—and Daniel was going to be too busy to listen.

Maddie vowed to make sure she had time. That wasn't interfering, exactly. Just being a friend. She had a feeling that this man needed a friend more than he needed anything else in the world, and if there was one thing she was good at, it was being a friend.

'How's your tea?' she asked, and he blinked and looked down into the mug.

'Fine—well, I assume it was. It's gone.'

She laughed softly. 'Can't have been too grim, then. Another?'

He shook his head. 'No. I just need to unload my stuff from the car and then get back to the hospital. I promised Angel I wouldn't be more than an hour, and the time's ebbing away. I mustn't be late.'

Maddie nodded, knowing how important it was to children in hospital that their parents could be trusted. 'I'm sure they'll be down soon—ah.'

The sound of the key in the door had her on her feet, and Robert followed her into the tiny sitting room. Daniel and Annie were there, arms round each other's waists, looking guilty and proud and ecstatically happy, and Maddie felt her eyes fill.

'Well?' she said impatiently, dying to hear them confirm her suspicions.

Daniel lifted his head and gave them a crooked grin. 'We're getting married,' he said, and all hell broke loose.

'I promised you I'd be back,' Robert said softly, and Angel sniffed and snuggled closer.

'I thought you'd forgotten.'

'No. I was back within an hour, but you were asleep. I didn't want to wake you. Maybe I should have done. I only went to grab a sandwich—I didn't think you'd wake up. I'm sorry, Angel.'

She wriggled even closer, her face hidden in his shirt so that the scars didn't show. She was so tiny— so small and fragile and dependent, with her long skinny limbs and fine, flyaway hair of darkest brown. He stroked it, feeling the baby softness of the strands, the ridge of scar tissue under the hair that ran from her eye back over her head and down by her ear.

That didn't matter, though. It was the other scars that worried her, criss-crossing her face, distorting her pretty mouth on one side, puckering her cheek. She needed this plastic surgery, really, but he didn't have the heart to put her through any more. The orthopaedics had been essential if she was to grow up without a significant limp, but this just seemed cosmetic, superficial—trivial compared to the fact that she was alive. Angel, though, didn't think it was trivial, and she'd gone on and on until he'd agreed. Now, he thought he must have been mad.

'Time you were asleep, young lady,' a nurse said, perching on the edge of the bed and smiling at them. 'Your dad needs to go home and get his beauty sleep, too, or he'll get bags under his eyes so big we'll be able to pack you inside them and carry you round!'

Angel gave a tiny smile and sat up, letting him go and turning to talk to the nurse. 'When can he come back?' she asked, a trace of anxiety still in her voice.

'As early as he likes. Some of the children wake up very early—about six or so? Others sleep longer. Shall we phone him when you wake up?'

Angel nodded, and Rob eased away from her and stood up. 'OK, darling. I'll wait for your call. You've got the mobile number?' he checked with the nurse, and she nodded.

'Yes. Don't worry, I'm sure we'll get hold of you.'

'I know the number anyway, Daddy,' Angel said in a slightly patronising voice much older than her six years, and he grinned.

'So you do.' He turned at the door of the ward and blew her a kiss, and she caught it and pressed it to her lips, her eyes serious over her hand. A silly little ritual, but part of their relationship, and one of the few things he felt he had left with her. If only she'd laugh again…

He'd left his car parked at Daniel's, so he went back there on foot, striding out briskly in the cold, clear night. It only took a matter of minutes, just long enough to feel the circulation stirring but not long enough to drive out the demons.

Maddie was in the hall, coming up from the basement with her keys in her teeth and her arms full of washing basket.

'You couldn't be a love and open my door again, could you?' she asked round the keys, and he grinned and took them from her and let her in, flicking the light switch and dropping the keys back onto the clothes in the basket.

'Tea?' she offered, but he shook his head.

'I need to get some sleep. Are they upstairs?'

'Yes.' Maddie's face looked worried. 'Rob, if you feel you're in the way up there, you can always camp here for a few days until you find somewhere—the sofa makes into a bed. It's nothing wonderful, but you're welcome, and I have a feeling Sarian won't be needing it.'

He nodded, wondering how he would feel with so much happiness bubbling all around him upstairs. 'Thanks, Maddie,' he murmured. 'I'll be all right. I can always go back to the hospital and pretend I was worried about Angel.'

'Pretend?' she said softly, and he pulled a wry face.

'OK, so I'm worried. I confess.'

She propped her shoulder against the wall and smiled sympathetically. 'It must be hell being a parent.'

'Especially when it's all your fault,' he said in an undertone, and turned on his heel, suddenly anxious to end this conversation before it started. 'I'll see you, Maddie.'

He went upstairs, pushing the light switches as he went, and stared at the keys Daniel had given him. He hesitated at the door, then knocked. A moment later it swung in and Daniel stood there. 'Hi. Come in. I thought I gave you some keys?'

'You did. I didn't like to use them,' Robert told him wryly, stepping inside.

His friend coloured slightly. 'Don't be silly. Anyway, Sarian's going in a minute. She's just finishing the washing-up—her turn, because I cooked. Have you eaten?'

'I grabbed something at the hospital,' he said, not wanting to get in the way and hoping the rather tired sandwich would see him through till the morning.

'OK. Let me show you your room.'

Daniel opened one of the doors off the sitting room, and Rob followed him into a pretty little bedroom, its ceiling sloping and quaint like the ceiling in the sitting room, only painted instead of being timber-clad in pale pine. It was simply furnished with twin beds, one each side of a pine chest, and there was a chair in one corner and a wardrobe against the wall, with his suitcase standing next to it. The window looked out over the city, with lights twinkling as far as the eye could see.

It all felt very familiar, reminding him of his time in London when he was training. The only difference was Easy, now changed almost beyond recognition by the happiness Sarian had brought into his life.

It contrasted sharply with the grief and guilt in Rob's own life, and brought it all into painful relief.

'Rob?'

He turned, meeting his friend's concerned eyes, and dredged up a smile. 'Thanks. It's fine.'

'Are you OK?'

He wasn't talking about the room, but Rob couldn't discuss what ailed him—most particularly not since it was his friend's fault! 'I'm fine, Easy,' he lied. 'Just worried about Angel.'

'She'll be OK. Gareth Davies will get her face sorted out—he's a genius. She'll be right as rain in no time.'

'I hope so.' He scrubbed a hand over his face and glanced at his watch. 'I think I'll turn in, actually. It's been a hell of a day.'

'Sure. I'll see you in the morning.'

'Daniel?'

'Yeah?'

'Sarian's not going home because of me, is she?'

His friend hesitated for a moment, then shook his head. 'Not really. We're trying to keep our engagement quiet for now, so it's not a bad idea. Anyway, there's no rush, we've got the rest of our lives.'

'I can go somewhere else, if you like. Maddie's offered me the sofa, or I can go back to the hospital and sleep there—they've offered me a bed.'

'No. You stay here—you're more than welcome, I meant it.'

'That was before Sarian.'

His smile was wry. 'Don't worry. I've waited thirty-two years for her, Rob. I can wait a little longer.' Daniel put a hand on his shoulder and squeezed lightly, then left, the door clicking quietly shut behind him. Robert heard Sarian's voice, then Daniel's, then a soft laugh followed by silence.

He was kissing her, Rob thought, and was shocked

by the ache of loneliness that the realisation brought. It was a familiar ache, though—all too familiar. He'd been lonely all his life, even during the six long years of his marriage. Perhaps lonelier then than he'd ever been.

He threw his coat down over the chair and stared out of the window at the lights in the distance. Daniel deserved to be happy. He'd had a hell of a life, with a father whose mind was warped by religious fervour and a mother too weak to stand up for her son—too weak or too indoctrinated by the tyrant that was her husband.

He heard the door of the flat open and close, then Daniel moving around for a while. Finally the flat was quiet, just the background roar of traffic and the sound of distant music to break the silence. He ought to go to bed. He was tired, it wasn't just a handy excuse to avoid company. He foraged about in his suitcase, came up with his wash things and a towel and went to look for the bathroom.

Sleep was a long time coming and then he woke at three, worried about Angel. Giving up, he washed and dressed quietly and slipped out of the door, and he was there in the chair when she woke at six.

'So, this is what I'm going to do while you're asleep—I'm going to get some paint, called Bonney's blue, and I'm going to draw on your face all the places I'm going to change, and then I'll take away all the old scar tissue and leave nice clean, healthy skin that will heal properly, and I'll sew it up with tiny tiny stitches and some very fine silk, and then we'll put a bandage on it and leave it alone for two or three weeks.'

'And then will I be pretty again?'

'Angel, you're pretty now,' Robert interrupted, but the surgeon ignored him.

'No. Not then. You'll still have fine bright pink lines where the skin's been cut, and for the first week you'll have sticky tape still, but then after that it will get better.'

'And then will I be pretty?'

'Yes,' he said firmly, and the child's shoulders sagged in relief, and her mouth curved up in a smile that tore at Robert's heart.

'Good,' she said quietly, and he could have wept.

Maddie glanced up from the white-board to see Robert walking slowly towards her. 'Hi there,' she said softly, and finished wiping out the name of her last patient. 'You look lost.'

He gave a hollow laugh. 'I am lost. Angel's in theatre.'

'Ah.' Maddie brushed off her hands and looked up at him searchingly. His eyes were shadowed and haunted, and she'd lay odds he'd hardly slept a wink. Poor man. Guilt was a dreadful thing, and she hadn't yet met the parent of an injured child that didn't suffer from guilt for one reason or another. 'Coffee?'

'Have you got time?'

She laughed without humour. 'Unbelievably, yes. There's nothing waiting that won't keep for a few moments, and the others can deal with them—anyway, I can pretend I'm giving you a guided tour ready for tomorrow. Actually, your timing's perfect.'

She led him down the corridor to the staff room, and put the kettle on. 'Have a seat. It's a bit basic in here, but it beats standing up in the corridor drinking the toxic waste from that machine out of a plastic cup. Tea or coffee?'

He smiled and sank into a chair with a groan. 'Coffee—not too strong, I've been OD-ing on it all morning. White, no sugar.'

'You can have decaf.' She pushed a tin across the table towards him. 'There might be some biscuits in there. Probably not any chocolate, they're always the first to go, but there might be some fruit shortcake.'

'Thanks.' She heard the tin lid scrape, then the steady munch of a biscuit disappearing. She made their coffee, helped herself to a biscuit and curled up in the chair across the corner from him, cradling her coffee gratefully. 'Oh, I'm glad you showed up. I didn't have a decent excuse to stop, and I've been dying for a coffee all morning!'

He gave a little grunt of laughter, then his expression turned serious again.

Maddie leant forwards and rested her hand lightly on his knee. 'Rob? She'll be all right, you know. Gareth Davies is brilliant.'

His eyes were racked with worry. 'I know. It's just so hard, when you love them. And it was all so unnecessary—'

He smacked his mug down on the table and stood up. 'I have to get back up there. She might be coming out of theatre soon.'

'Why don't you ring from here?' she suggested.

He shook his head. 'I'll go up. Thanks for your help, Maddie. I'll see you later.'

She stood up and followed him, worried by the strain he was under. 'Have you got any plans for tonight?' she asked softly.

He stopped and turned back. 'Plans? No—why?'

'I thought I might feed you. I don't suppose you've had a decent home-cooked meal in the last week.'

He snorted. 'Try month—or maybe year. I seem to be living on junk food and take-aways.'

'So will you come?'

He smiled tiredly. 'It sounds wonderfully tempting, but I can't leave Angel, Maddie—not tonight, of all nights.'

'Another time then—maybe over the weekend,' she suggested, and he made a noncommittal noise and went off to wait for his daughter, leaving Maddie to wonder why she felt so curiously disappointed...

CHAPTER TWO

MADDIE spent the rest of that long and difficult day thinking about Rob and his little daughter Angel. Angelique to be specific, she remembered, but he called her Angel as if she really were.

Maybe she was, to him. His guardian angel, perhaps, the thing that kept him sane and directed his life. Certainly she was the most important thing to him—more important probably than his own health or well-being, which ultimately would suffer unless he took better care of himself.

She glanced up at the clock at twelve-thirty, and wondered how Angel was getting on. Was she out of theatre yet? Probably not. Was it going smoothly?

A new arrival claimed her attention for a while, a boy with a truly spectacular greenstick fracture following a fall from a garden wall.

He was crying, with that terrible keening wail of real pain, and she called the orthopaedic registrar down straight away. While they waited for him Daniel looked briefly at it, ordered X-rays and bloods for cross match just in case, and by the time the orthopaedic registrar appeared, the boy was X-rayed, his arm was propped up and he was much more comfortable having been given painkillers.

'Theatre, I think,' the young woman said with a wince, looking at the distorted arm and the pictures. She smiled at Darren's mother, then quickly examined the little fingers. They were discoloured, and it was clear that the circulation and possibly the nerve supply had been disrupted.

'I think, my love, we need to send you to sleep for a few minutes so we can straighten your arm up and get it all comfy again—OK?'

He moaned sleepily, and his mother leant forwards in her chair, clearly agitated. 'Is it bad?' she asked worriedly.

'Well, it's not good, but we can deal with it. It's quite a common sort of fracture and we usually get a very good result. Theatre should be free soon, so we can prep him and get him up there as quickly as possible. When did he last eat?'

'Oh—just a light breakfast,' his mother said. 'I was just going to call him in for lunch when I heard him cry out. He should have been at school today, but he felt a bit sick this morning.'

'Not so sick he couldn't climb the wall,' the doctor said drily, and Maddie hid a smile. Yet another skiving child that would have been better off not pretending to be sick!

She made the boy comfortable again, put another blanket over him because he was beginning to feel cold with shock, and shortly afterwards he was dispatched to theatre.

Then a little girl called Cara came in following a playground accident, and Maddie gently took the covering off her cheek and winced. 'Oh, sweetheart, you've made a bit of a mess of that, haven't you?' she said softly. It was filthy, a nasty jagged tear and scrape full of grit and dirt, and would need debriding under anaesthetic and probably the attention of a plastic surgeon.

'The next time you want to lie down in the playground, I suggest you stop running first,' Maddie teased, and the little girl gave a tearful giggle.

'I didn't want to lie down,' she told Maddie firmly. 'I wanted to win the race.'

'And did you?'

'Almost,' she said sorrowfully. 'But Stevie pushed me over. He wanted to win.'

'Well, then, I should say you probably were the winner,' Maddie assured her. 'Cheating doesn't count.'

And hopefully one little boy's ambition wouldn't have scarred her for life. She called Daniel in, then they contacted the plastics team and Peggie O'Neill came down and tutted and said, 'Oh, dear, what a grubby face you've got there now,' and agreed that she would have to go up to theatre.

'We'll give your face the best wash it's ever had in its life,' the young Irishwoman told Cara and her mother. 'And then we'll stick it all back together again so nobody will ever know!'

Rather her than me, Maddie thought to herself as she followed the doctor out of the cubicle. She knew they'd have to scrub out the dirty wound with fine wire brushes and antiseptic, and if the slightest trace of grit was left in, the scar would be 'tattooed' with the dirt.

However, despite the attention she was paying to little Cara, her thoughts were still with Robert's daughter, and she followed Peggie down the corridor a little way so they could talk quietly. 'Peggie, do you know if Angelique Oliver's out of theatre yet?'

'Angel? Yes, she is. Do you know her?'

'Her father—he's starting work here tomorrow. I just wondered how it had gone.'

'Oh, excellent, I think. Gareth was very pleased in the end, but it was quite tricky. Luckily the first surgeon hadn't done any damage, so she was a good candidate. They'd left the wound clean, used small enough stitches and thankfully she hadn't gone through the windscreen, but I think at the time from what I've gathered her face was the least of her worries. Pity about her leg, but maybe they'll be able to do something more later.'

Her leg? Not another problem, Maddie thought in dismay. What was wrong with her leg?

She didn't have time to worry, because the department had one of those mad fits where they were running out of chairs and couldn't keep up with the constant flow. Then an RTA came in, a boy who had been knocked off his bike on the way home from school, and it got even worse.

Daniel was working flat out in Resus alongside Annie, and at one point when Maddie stuck her head round the door Daniel grinned and said, 'Pity Rob didn't start today. We could do with another pair of hands.'

She gave a humourless laugh. 'I don't think there's any danger he'll leave Angel. You'll just have to carry on being in two places at once. Where's Tim today?'

'Day off,' Daniel said succinctly, sliding a needle home and connecting up a drip. 'All we need is this traffic jam in the waiting room.'

'I'll do some triage and get rid of a few of them to their GPs,' Maddie said with a laugh. 'I'm sure they can't all be genuine.'

Jenny Barber helped her, and to their dismay there were only two who truly didn't need to be there.

Some the nurses could deal with themselves—nasty grazes, cuts that needed a little stitch, a splinter, a blood blister under a nail—but others needed the doctors, and they had to wait until Daniel's patient was stable and on his way to theatre before he could attend to them.

It was the end of her shift before Maddie got two minutes to herself, and she dumped her colourful tabard in the laundry bin, pulled her coat out of her locker and paused.

She didn't have to go anywhere or do anything. Nobody was expecting her at home. She could go up to the ward and see little Cara, to find out how she was getting on—and if Robert was there, she could ask about Angel without it looking as if she was following him.

She stuffed the coat back in her locker, turned the key and headed for the lift.

He was aware of her presence long before he saw her. There was just a quietness, an aura of comfort, that radiated from her. He enjoyed it for a moment before turning slowly towards her.

'Hi.' His voice sounded rusty, unused.

'Hi. How is she?'

'She's fine, apparently. It's gone well. Gareth's back in theatre—he's had an emergency that put things back.'

'I know, I came up to see her. She had an accident in the playground—lots of grit in her face.' Her voice was soft and melodious, the opposite of his, soothing and comforting and gentle. He wanted to make her talk, just to hear it.

She perched on Angel's bed, one soft, feminine hip

hitched up, her thighs only a foot away from him as he sat by the bed. He had a crazy urge to bury his face in her lap and howl, but he couldn't. How he needed her comfort, though!

Angel stirred, mumbling something, and he leant towards her, forgetting about Maddie. 'It's all right, darling, Daddy's here,' he said, taking her tiny hand in his and squeezing gently.

Her fingers flickered in response, and he kissed them, pressing them against his cheek. Please, God, let her be all right, he prayed. Let her not hurt too much—let it work. Don't let her scar again.

'Daddy?' Her voice was muffled by the bandages, the layers of paraffin gauze and wool and crêpe that would hold her face still until it had healed. Her eyes flickered open, bleary and unfocussed, and he leant forwards and kissed the tip of her nose, just visible through the dressings.

'Hello, my pretty little Angel—how are you?'

'Am I pretty?' she asked sleepily.

'Of course you are.' His heart contracted. She'd always be pretty to him, but she seemed obsessed, and his guilt plagued him. 'You're gorgeous, but at the moment you should be sleeping.'

'In a minute,' she mumbled a little drunkenly. 'Will you love me now I'm pretty?'

'I do love you, sweetheart,' he assured her desperately. Oh, God, what was wrong with her? She was so insecure, so withdrawn since the accident. 'You know I love you—I'll always love you, and being pretty's nothing to do with it.'

'But what if I'm not your pretty little Angel?' she asked, her little voice unsteady and agitated. 'Will you still love me?'

'Of course—but you are.'

'If I'm pretty maybe you'll still be my daddy.'

He was stunned. Where had that come from? 'Of course I'll be your daddy. I'll always be your daddy. You can't change that.'

'Mummy said you weren't my daddy. She said it was easy. She said you didn't love us so we had to live with Carlos.'

Blinding rage flooded him, but he clamped it down, as he always clamped it down. Maria was dead—it was finished. 'That's nonsense,' he said firmly, denying any possibility that she might be right. 'Of course I'm your daddy, and even if I wasn't, it wouldn't make any difference. I still love you, and I always will. Now go to sleep, sweetheart, and stop worrying. I'll see you when you wake up.'

'Will you be here?' she mumbled, drifting off.

'Yes,' he assured her, and wondered if he would be able to start work the next day or not. Probably not, if she continued to be so clingy and worried. Oh, Lord. He was going to have to cut himself up so he could be everywhere at once.

He pressed his lips to her hand and laid it down, keeping his fingers curled around hers. Gradually they relaxed, the tension seeping out of her, and a soft snore escaped from the bandages.

He felt a light hand on his shoulder. 'Robert?'

He looked up, into gentle, compassionate eyes, and felt emotion welling in him. 'Why would she tell her a thing like that?' he asked under his breath.

'Do you want to talk about it?'

He looked at Angel, fast asleep now. 'Not here. Not now.'

'Let me feed you.'

'I can't leave her.'

'Rob, she's asleep. She won't wake for ages now.'

He shook his head. 'I still can't. I promised.'

Maddie rolled her eyes. 'Rob, look at you!' she said in an urgent undertone. 'You're exhausted! You've been sitting about all day worrying about her, and now you know she's all right. You've got to relax. You've got to take time for you or you won't be there for her. You'll collapse. It's not just today—it's been going on for months and months, hasn't it?'

A soft footfall made him raise his head, and Daniel came into view over Maddie's shoulder.

'How is she?'

'OK,' he said mechanically.

Maddie turned to Daniel. 'Daniel, he has to eat something and walk around for a while or he'll turn into a zombie. Talk sense into him.'

Daniel's eyes tracked over his face and he shook his head. 'You look like hell, old friend. Do as the lady says—go and have a meal in the canteen and stretch your legs—and stop drinking so much coffee. I'll stay with her till you get back in case she wakes up. She knows me.'

Robert gave in. He knew when he was outnumbered. He stood up stiffly, stretching his neck and shoulders, and dropped a hand on Daniel's shoulder.

'You're a good friend, Easy,' he said quietly. 'I won't be long. We'll be in the canteen.'

Maddie stood up. 'No, we'll be in the Newt and Cucumber,' she corrected. 'They do the best bar snacks in London, and it's just next door. Daniel will ring if you're needed.'

'I've got my mobile—the ward staff have got the number.'

He let her lead him out of the ward, looking once over his shoulder to check that Angel was still asleep, and seeing his friend settle into the chair and pick up her hand.

'Mummy said you weren't my daddy. She said it was easy.'

What was easy?

Or had she said Easy? Was that what Maria had meant? That Daniel, and not he, was her father? Bile clawed at him.

'Excuse me,' he muttered, and, diving into the nearest loo, he lost the meagre contents of his stomach.

'Are you all right?'

He nodded, but Maddie didn't believe him. He looked pale and shaken, as if something drastic had just happened. He looked in fact as if he was in shock, and Maddie thought back over what Angel had said. She hadn't heard all of it, and some she hadn't been able to understand, but Robert's replies had filled in some of the gaps. Had his wife told the child that he wasn't her father? And if so, why? And if it was the case, had he known but thought the child didn't know?

'Come on,' she said firmly, giving up on that for now. 'You need to eat.'

'Oh, God, no,' he groaned, but she shook her head and took his arm.

'Oh, God, yes. You need food, you need to sit down and get everything off your chest, and you need sleep. We can go in the pub—it's nice and noisy so we can talk without being overheard, and you can have as little or as much to eat as you want, but you will eat, and you will talk, and you will feel better.'

His mouth kicked up in a crooked smile. 'Yes, Mother,' he said obediently, and she smiled back, ruthlessly crushing the urge to hug him. He wouldn't appreciate it now. He didn't know her well enough.

They went out of the front of the hospital and round the corner, up a little side road to an old-fashioned pub with wooden chairs and a dartboard and the best food in the area, if not in London. They found a table in the corner, by a miracle, and Maddie pushed him down into a chair and fetched a jug of iced water, two glasses and a menu.

'Right. Drink that, and look at the menu, and then tell me what happened in there.'

He gave a short, bitter laugh. 'Just like that? Seven years of hell summed up in a sentence?'

'I've got all night,' she said softly, and his face seemed to crumple.

'I don't know where to start,' he said unevenly.

'How about the beginning?'

'Hi, Maddie.'

She looked up at the young waitress, the mother of a one-time patient, and smiled, mentally cursing her timing. 'Hi, Jane. How are you both?'

'Fine. Great. Are you ready to order?' she asked, flipping the top sheet of her notebook over.

Maddie glanced at Robert, his face white and strained, his mouth a tight line, and shook her head. 'No. Actually I don't think we'll be eating here tonight, thank you, Jane. Maybe another time.'

She stood up. 'Come on. We'll go to my flat. It's only five minutes' walk to the hospital. We'll ring and tell them where we are.'

'No need—I've got my mobile with me. They'll ring if she wakes.'

'OK.' They walked briskly along the lighted streets, their breath misting on the cold night air, and Maddie ushered him into her sitting room, went and put the kettle on and some toast in, then went back.

He was standing by the window, turning a little ornament over in his hands, staring blindly at it. As she went back in he set it down very, very carefully on the shelf and looked out of the window.

'Robert?' she said softly.

'I don't even know if she's my daughter,' he said raggedly. 'All these years, and suddenly I find out that she may be—' He broke off, his jaw working, and suddenly Maddie didn't care any longer whether he'd like it or resent it—she just knew he needed a hug.

'Poor baby,' she said, and, walking up to him, she held out her arms and enfolded him in their embrace. For a moment he stood there rigidly, and then with a muffled groan he wrapped his arms around her and clung on tight. His shoulders heaved under her hands, but he hung on, dragging in great lungfuls of air, and after a moment he eased away and scrubbed his hands over his face.

'I'm sorry. I don't know what happened,' he said gruffly.

'I do. You reached the end of your tether,' she told him, and led him to the kitchen. 'Let's have some tea and toast. It's not quite the meal I promised you, but I think you need to talk more than you need anything else.'

She pushed him into a chair, set a pile of toast and two plates down in front of him and made tea while he buttered the toast. Then she sat down opposite, pushed a mug across the table towards him and took him back to the beginning.

'How did you meet her?' she asked.

He took a deep breath and let it out on a sigh. 'She was going out with Daniel. He was held up at the hospital, and so I invited her in and offered her a glass of wine. I had to—I was halfway down the bottle and had no intention of stopping. It was one of those bloody awful weeks when everything goes wrong. I'd just lost a patient, a young woman who had no business dying, and I was drowning my sorrows.'

Maddie took a piece of toast. 'We've all done it.'

'Absolutely. Anyway, Daniel rang just as we started the next bottle, and said he wasn't coming home—he had an emergency. Maria started to cry, and I comforted her, and one thing led to another and the next thing I knew she came round to tell me she was pregnant.'

'Oops.'

'Yes, oops. She said it was mine—she said she hadn't slept with Daniel, that he wouldn't, but she was a good Catholic girl from an old Portuguese family and her father would kill her.'

'So you married her?'

He nodded. 'Yes. I married her, and Angel was born, and for a while it wasn't too bad considering we were total strangers. Then we started to fight—just every now and again at first, then more and more, until in the end every evening ended with a screaming match.'

His jaw worked, and he swallowed, looking down and playing with the toast on his plate. 'She used to yell at me, and Angel would run to me and cry, and I'd try and reason with Maria and keep calm which just infuriated her even more. She used to throw things at us—vases, plates, anything she could lay her hands on, and then she'd storm off and lock herself in the bedroom and leave me to deal with Angel.'

'Poor little girl,' Maddie murmured, wondering what it must be like to have parents who fought. Her own parents always had been, and still were, blissfully happy together.

'I used to put her to bed and stay with her until I was too cold or cramped to lie on the edge of her little bed any more, then I'd go and lie on the settee, or sometimes if Maria had unlocked the bedroom door I'd go to bed and lie there and wonder if this was how the rest of our lives were going to be, and how long we could go on hating each other so much.'

'Why didn't you just get divorced?' Maddie asked.

He snorted. 'She was a Catholic, remember? Good Catholics don't get divorced. They don't get drunk and sleep with strangers either, but it was too late to worry about that.'

Maddie bit into the toast again, chewing thoughtfully as she mulled over what he'd told her so far. 'So—what happened to change it all?' she asked eventually.

He sighed. 'I don't know. Her cousin came over to London on business and looked her up. I suppose that must have been the beginning. She started going back to Portugal every now and then, sometimes on her own, sometimes taking Angel, and then she went back there last April and I had a letter saying she was staying there with Angel and not coming back.'

'Just like that, without any warning?'

'Absolutely. I rang several times, but her mother said she didn't know where she was, and in the end she told me to leave them alone. So I went over there and looked for her.' He blew a bubble across the top of his tea absently, his gaze fixed on a place she couldn't see, and finally he started speaking again.

'It was her cousin, strangely enough, who told me where she was. Afterwards I wondered why he was so helpful—if he was hoping I'd take her back to England, if perhaps everything had gone sour. Whatever, he lent me his car and sent me off into the hills. She was staying in his villa.'

'His villa? So were they having an affair?'

He nodded. 'Apparently. Anyway, when I turned up out of the blue Maria was furious. We had a row, and she told me she was going back to Carlos, this cousin. She told Angel to get into the car and I didn't worry because I had the keys in my pocket, but it was Carlos' car, and of course she had keys.'

He looked up at her, his eyes tortured by guilt and pain and misery. 'She lost control at the bottom of the drive—there was a lorry coming, and she swerved round it and spun off the road and down the ravine. Angel was flung clear, thank God, but Maria was trapped in the car. It exploded at the bottom.'

There were times when Maddie wished she didn't have such a vivid imagination, and this was one of them. She could just picture the car tumbling down the hillside, hear the child screaming, hear the roar of the explosion—and Robert—what had he felt? Had he seen it happen?

He went on in a dull monotone. 'I've never felt so helpless. It took me an hour to find Angel. She was stuck in a tree, her legs bent up in the branches, her face torn to ribbons. They got her out in the end by putting ladders down to the tree and carrying her out, then she was taken to hospital.'

Once again, Maddie could picture the scene, and

the terrified, sobbing child. 'Was she conscious?' she asked, hoping the answer would be no.

'Some of the time. She kept drifting in and out, and she wouldn't let go of my hand. They did what they could—cleaned up her face, mended her legs to restore the circulation, and then we flew home, but it took nearly a year and several more operations to sort her out to the point she's at now.'

'And Maria?' Maddie asked gently.

He gave a ragged sigh. 'They had to cut Maria's body out of the car when the fire had cooled, but she'd had a massive head injury so she was probably already dead when it hit the bottom. I hope so. Whatever else I might have felt about her, I wouldn't have wanted that for her. I never wanted her to die. She was just as much a victim of the whole thing as I was.'

Maddie brushed the tears from her eyes and sniffed. 'I'm sorry. It must have been so hard for you.'

'Not as hard as it was for Angel. She's the one who's really suffered in all this. Maria can't have known anything about it very much, and I—'

'Yes?' she prompted. 'What about you? You saw your wife killed and your daughter horribly injured. Don't you think you suffered?'

He gave a harsh laugh and pushed the plate of toast away, virtually untouched. 'Not really. Probably not as much as I should have done. It was my fault, Maddie. I caused it. If I hadn't slept with her out of drunken curiosity, if I hadn't married her and made her life hell, if I'd been a better husband—if I hadn't followed her up the mountain and tried to persuade her to come back...'

'So many "if"'s, Rob,' Maddie said softly. 'Maria

had choices too, you know. She was there when you made love. She wanted to marry you. She fought with you. She went to Portugal and started an affair with her cousin—and she drove the car off the road.'

Maddie leant forwards and gripped his hand.

'She was a responsible adult, Robert. It was every bit as much her fault as yours, all of it. And the crash was her fault. You couldn't have known she had keys, and she should have known better than to go so fast.'

His shoulders drooped, and he turned his hand over and gripped hers, his thumb absently grazing the skin as he stroked it back and forth. 'Maybe you're right, Maddie, but I still feel guilty, and I'll feel guilty every time I look at my daughter's face.'

'And does it show in your eyes? Do you look at her with pity, and does she see that and wonder if she's ugly to you?'

He buried his face in his hands. 'I don't know,' he mumbled. 'I just know I love her more than I can begin to say, and now I don't even know if she's mine, or if she's—'

'Whose?'

He lifted his head and his eyes were bleak and filled with pain.

'Daniel's.'

CHAPTER THREE

ROBERT spent that night back at the hospital beside his daughter, and Maddie spent the night lying curled on her side, tears trickling down into her pillow, wondering how he could bear everything that had happened to them.

And to have to wonder if his best friend was the father of his child...

'You've got to ask him,' she'd said, but he'd shaken his head emphatically.

'No. She told me at the time they hadn't been having an affair, and if they had, I'm sure he'd have told me.'

'But what if he hadn't? What if he'd not wanted to interfere with your happiness?'

'He knew why we were getting married. He knew there was no question of happy ever after—I never hid anything from him.'

'Maybe he wasn't so open. Maybe he didn't know how to tell you.'

But Rob had shaken his head in denial. Maybe he needed to leave his relationship with Daniel intact, and to challenge him, to ask again about his relationship with Maria, would show a lack of trust that she felt Rob would find even harder to deal with than the uncertainty about Angel's parentage.

Whatever his reasoning, he'd refused to discuss it any further. In truth, Maddie was amazed he'd discussed as much as he had, but he'd obviously needed to open up. She'd managed to get some of the toast into him and another cup of tea, before duty had dragged him up to the flat for a change of clothes and then back to the hospital.

An hour later Daniel and Sarian had come back, and Maddie found herself looking at him curiously and wondering.

It's none of your business, she told herself again and again. Nothing to do with you. Butt out.

But nothing could stop her thinking about Rob and his little girl, or crying herself to sleep. She overslept, of course, and had to rush. Sarian was on the bed settee when she woke up, but she was on a late again and Maddie was on an early, and if she didn't get a move on she wouldn't be there till long after the shift started.

She dressed hastily, forgot about breakfast and ran to the hospital, arriving at two minutes past seven out of breath and starving.

'Afternoon,' Charity sang out cheekily, and Maddie poked her tongue out at the tall young staff nurse.

'And hello to you, too,' she said, stuffing her coat into her locker without ceremony. 'Anything happening?'

'Dunno. I only just got here myself. Shall we go and find out?'

They walked down the corridor together, Charity giving Maddie sideways looks, until in the end she stopped and put her hands on her hips and sighed. 'What is it?'

'You look tired. You've got purple smudges under your eyes. You need more sleep.'

Maddie eyed Charity's smooth, near-black skin with disgust. 'It's easy for you to say that—you can

stay up all night and get away with it, with that flawless skin. I only have to miss ten minutes' sleep and
I look like a bag lady.'

Charity chuckled deliciously. 'Oh, Maddie, don't
be so silly. You've got beautiful skin. You just look
tired.' Her face sobered. 'Are you really OK?'

Maddie smiled at her and patted her arm. 'Charity,
I'm fine, I just didn't sleep very well. Just feed me
coffee if I start to slide down the wall.'

They went into the office and found the night sister
writing up a report. 'Hi—anything exciting going
on?' Maddie asked.

She rolled her eyes and flexed her shoulders. 'Are
you kidding? It's been chaos all night, and about six
o'clock it all settled down again. I don't know why
you get so lucky.'

'Yesterday was hell,' Maddie reminded her.

'And today you've got the new man starting—
Robert Oliver. Have you met him yet?'

Maddie felt a little rush of warmth glide over her
colourless face, and wondered if it showed. 'Um—
yes. He's a friend of Daniel Burr. He's staying in the
flat with Daniel, so I've seen quite a bit of him. His
daughter's just had an operation here.'

'I know. He rang. She's had a bad night, I gather.
She's been in a lot of pain, and they've had to sedate
her quite heavily. I don't think he'll be much use to
us today—I suggest if you have time you let him ease
in and get the feel of the place. Talk to Tim and
Maureen when they come in. As for the rest, we don't
have anybody left in the unit at the moment, amazingly. Long may it continue. Right, I'm going home.
Spiro's around somewhere—bleep him if you
need him.'

And she left them to it.

'I wonder how long it'll be this quiet?' Charity murmured, and the phone began to ring.

'That long,' Maddie said with a laugh. 'You shouldn't have spoken.'

Then the doors opened and a young woman ran in with her baby in her arms, a man hard on her heels, and Maddie forgot about Angel's bad night and Robert starting shortly, and just concentrated on the job.

'Can I help you?' she said, moving towards the group.

'She can't breathe,' the woman said frantically. 'She's fighting for breath, but she can't seem to drag it in!'

Maddie took the baby straight into Resus, telling Charity to call Spiro stat, and laid her down on the examination couch, propping the backrest up at forty five degrees. Far from not being able to breathe in, it seemed the baby couldn't breathe out—a classic case of asthma, possibly, or maybe an inhaled foreign body or bronchiolitis.

'Have any of you got asthma, hay fever or any other allergies?' Maddie asked, reaching for the humidified oxygen.

'I have hay fever,' the father said, 'but nothing like this.'

'Anything changed in the house? A new pet, carpet, flowers, air freshener, washing powder—'

'A carpet. A new carpet in the lounge about four weeks ago, but she was lying on it last night.'

'Wool?' Maddie asked, wishing Spiro would turn up.

'A mixture.'

'That might be it. Otherwise is there anything she could have put in her mouth and breathed in—a pen top, or a little toy, or anything like that?' Oh, Spiro, where are you? she thought, and then the door swung open and Rob strode in.

'Can I help?'

'Baby girl, query asthma. First attack.'

'Given her anything?'

'A hundred per cent humidified oxygen.'

'OK. Let's give her some nebulized salbutamol, and intravenous aminophylline.'

They worked together on her, while the parents stood at her head and stroked her and the mother cried, and then after a few more nerve-racking moments Spiro turned up. They worked together for a while longer until she was stabilised, and then the baby was moved out to ITU for further treatment and they could all relax.

Maddie turned to Rob and gave him a weary smile. 'Thanks,' she murmured, and then she looked at his face.

Good grief, she thought, if Charity thought I looked tired, what would she say about our new registrar?

'How's Angel?' she asked quietly, busying herself with the clearing up so she wouldn't wrap him in her arms and hug him better, as she wanted to. 'I gather she had a bad night.'

He scrubbed his hands through his hair and sighed. 'You could say that. I think I got about ten minutes' sleep in twenty or so increments.'

Maddie laughed softly, steeling herself against too much sympathy. There were times when it wasn't necessary or appropriate—times when positive action was better. This was one.

'Coffee,' she said firmly, 'decaf, so you don't ping off the walls, and lots of biscuits. I don't want you drooping on me halfway through the day. I've got enough problems keeping myself awake.'

'I think I need rocket fuel, not decaf and fruit short-cake.'

'We've got chocolate butter crunch today,' she tempted, crossing her fingers that the night staff hadn't pigged the lot.

He brightened visibly. 'Sounds good. Lead the way, Sister.'

He followed her down the corridor and into the staff room at the end, and while she made the coffee he slumped into one of the more comfortable chairs and propped his feet up on the edge of the table. A magazine slid to the floor and he glowered at it half-heartedly.

Maddie scooped it up, dropped it back on the pile by his feet and plonked the coffee mug on top. 'Here. Drink, and have a few biscuits. They haven't got them all yet.'

She thrust the tin towards him, and he fished out a couple and munched them quietly, eyes closed.

'You look awful,' she said without thinking, and one eye cracked open and regarded her steadily.

'I feel much better for knowing that.'

She felt herself colour. 'I'm sorry. I had no right to say that, but you do look very tired.'

'I *am* very tired. It's all right for Angel, of course, because she's gone back to sleep now and she's out for the count. It's the rest of us that have to cope.' He gave a short laugh. 'Still, it's hardly her fault. It was hurting her. I think all the layers of tulle and wool and bandages must feel very odd.'

Maddie nodded, tucking her feet under her bottom and shoving her nose into her coffee mug. It smelt wonderful. She could stay there all day, sniffing it and drowsing gently.

'Have you had breakfast?' he asked her.

She laughed without humour. 'No. I overslept. Chuck us a biscuit.'

'Why don't we go and have some? It's quiet, and you can bet your life it won't last. We might as well grab the chance—'

'Maddie? Emergency coming in,' Charity said, sticking her head round the door. She threw a grin at Rob. 'You must be the new guy—welcome to the madhouse.'

His mouth kicked up in an automatic smile. 'Thank you—I think,' he murmured. He caught Maddie's eye, and the tired smile became wry. 'So much for breakfast.'

'They serve it until eleven. Then it turns into lunch.'

'I'll treat you—whenever it is. I shall remain optimistic about our chances of getting some—otherwise I'll start chewing the furniture.'

'Down, Rover,' Maddie said softly, and he chuckled and stood up.

'I suppose we ought to go and deal with this emergency.'

Maddie hoisted herself to her feet, sighed regretfully at her half-finished mug of coffee and followed him back to the coalface.

'So, how's Angel now?'

Rob shrugged at Maddie and stabbed a prawn with a fork. 'Still asleep, I gather. I rang the ward half an hour ago and she was out for the count. She must be feeling better—or doped.'

'Or both. Have you decided what you're going to do about accommodation?'

He sighed. 'Not really. Daniel tells me I'm not in the way, but they're in the first throes of this wonderful romance—they need time alone, even if they don't want to live together until they're married, and I just feel like a spare part.' He prodded his salad half-heartedly. 'So, no, I haven't decided what to do, just that I should do something. Why?'

Maddie stole a prawn from his salad and made yum noises for a moment, then tipped her head on one side and watched the man who dealt with staff accommodation cross the room. Now, there was an idea. 'How about living in the hospital? If Angel's got to spend the next few weeks in here, you need to be close.'

'But I can't sleep on a cot by her bed indefinitely—'

'No—the flats. There are dedicated staff flats available. I think they're quite reasonable, not huge but quite pleasant. They've got a bedroom and sitting room, a shower room, and a communal kitchen on each floor, if I remember right, and it would give you time to find something else for you and Angel once she's out of hospital.'

He nodded slowly, thoughtfully, and then looked up at her. 'Any chance there's one free?'

She shrugged. 'I don't know. There often is. Go and see the man over there, in the green shirt—'

He glanced across the room in the direction that she was brandishing her fork, shot his chair back and stood up. 'Back in a mo.'

He went over to the man and they had a brief exchange while Maddie filched another prawn, and he came back and smiled apologetically. 'Sorry, I have to go and see his secretary. There might be a flat available. I'm going to find out now.'

She prodded his plate. 'Do you want your salad?'

'No. You have it—you've had half the prawns already anyway. It's a bit early for me. It's only twelve now.'

'You should be more flexible,' she teased. She grinned, pulled the plate towards her and polished off the remaining prawns, then picked her way through the lettuce and tomato. She'd already had her own meal, but she wasn't going to let it go to waste.

Just waist, instead. Oh, darn.

She pushed the plate away, but not before finding the last hidden prawn and popping it in her mouth. She had a feeling he wouldn't reappear until he'd seen the accommodation, if there was any, but she was wrong.

He was back a few minutes later, just as she was about to go back to the department, and he strode over with a key dangling from one lean, long finger. 'Coming?'

It was the nearest to animated she'd ever seen him, and she realised then just how much he missed his independence and privacy, even in so few days. She glanced at her watch and stood up. 'If we're quick.'

'We'll be quick. Do you know the way?'

She grinned. 'I knew you wanted me for a reason.'

'Of course,' he said easily. 'What else?'

What else indeed? Maddie thought. The day a man wanted her for herself would be a miracle—and especially a man like Rob.

'So, if they're so good, why aren't you living in one of these flats?' Rob asked as they walked briskly along the corridor.

'Me? I value my privacy and independence too much,' she said with a laugh. 'I already feel as if I live here. If I really did, I think I'd go round the bend. Anyway, I like cooking and I couldn't bear sharing a kitchen.'

'That's not going to be a problem for me,' Rob said. 'I can burn water. In fact, I might have to take you up on your offer of a home-cooked meal one day, just to stop me going crazy.'

'My pleasure,' she said with a smile. 'Just tell me when.'

'When Angel stops being so unpredictable,' he said drily.

'Do you want to check on her again, by the way?'

'I should, but she seems to sense my arrival. Knowing my luck she'll wake up just as I have to go and deal with an emergency.'

Maddie thought it quite likely, but with Tim and Daniel both in the department as well that day, it probably wouldn't matter. They reached the door at the back of the hospital, and followed the wide gravel path that led to the entrance of the flats.

'There's a security lock on the door—he gave me the code,' Rob muttered, peering at something written on the back of his hand. He punched in some numbers, and the door opened, revealing a common entrance-way with a pay phone and a notice-board.

'It's upstairs, on the left, apparently. Let's see if we can find it.'

Maddie followed Rob up the stairs, and at the top he veered left through a pair of glass doors, slid a key into the lock of the first door off the corridor and swung it open.

She peered over his shoulder, scanning the bleak, empty flatlet, devoid of any humanising touches, and wondered what he would make of it. He was quiet, opening doors, checking the bed squeezed in between functional cabinets, a wall of fitted cupboards opposite the foot giving storage, the shower room, small but providing all that was necessary, and then came back into the living room and looked round again.

It was clean enough, but so barren, so institutional, so bleak.

'It's fine,' he said, and Maddie ached for him. How sad, that this bare, empty, soulless flat was fine.

'It needs a bit of colour—some cushions, a rug, plants.'

He shrugged. 'I just want somewhere to sleep, Maddie. I won't be here much. Angel will need me before her bedtime, and I'll need to be up early to see her at the beginning of the day. No, it'll do fine until she's out of hospital and we need something bigger.'

And what about you? she thought sadly. What about what you need?

They went back to the main hospital block, parting at the door. Maddie went back to A and E, and Rob went to secure his accommodation and see his daughter before he had to be back at work. She watched him go, glancing over her shoulder as he strode away, his shoulders squared as if he dreaded the coming ordeal of seeing his daughter so bandaged and helpless.

He needed someone to help him—someone to share the burden, to talk to, to make life easier. She wondered when he'd move into his flat, and how Daniel would take the news.

Secretly, she thought he'd be pleased, although he was bound to protest that it was unnecessary.

Whatever. She went into the staff room, put the kettle on and glanced at Charity, sprawled in a chair with her feet up, flicking through a magazine. 'Coffee?' she offered.

Charity dropped the magazine and grinned. 'Could do. Things are slow. Maybe I'll get time to drink it today. So, how was lunch with the gorgeous Dr Oliver?'

Maddie laughed a little self-consciously. 'He wasn't there for half of it. He's taking a hospital flat— we went and had a look.'

'Is it nice? I've never been in one.'

She wrinkled her nose. 'Bare, basic. It could be nice. It's just a bit institutional—it's got the essentials, I suppose, and it's only temporary, while Angel's in hospital.'

'What's only temporary?'

She swivelled round and stared guiltily at Daniel. Damn. Perhaps Rob should have told Daniel first, before she started discussing his business with the rest of the department. Still, it was too late now. She hastily explained, 'Rob's just looked at a hospital flat— Angel needs him close at the moment, and he can't sleep in a chair or on a little camp bed for weeks.'

Daniel nodded. 'I wondered. He said something yesterday about not wanting to be so far from her. Sounds like a good idea. What's it like?'

So she repeated her 'basic' comment, described the simple facilities and then the phone rang. She scooped it up, and it was Rob, ringing to say Angel was awake and could he speak to Daniel.

'Sure. Daniel, for you. Rob.'

She handed the phone over, pushed a coffee at Daniel and carried hers and Charity's over to the corner, then sat down next to her.

'Strong, black and sweet, just how I'd like my man,' Charity said, then added with a laugh, 'if I ever get that lucky!'

Maddie chuckled, one ear on the conversation Daniel was having. It sounded as if he was encouraging Rob to take the rest of the day off, and his next words confirmed that Tim had approved it.

He turned to Maddie and smiled wryly. 'He's trapped. She won't let him go, and he's too soft to leave her. He's going to pick his stuff up tonight if he can get away, and move into the flat. I've told him he owes me for this afternoon.'

Maddie nodded, returning his smile. 'I'm sure he's grateful—and I'm sure it was the last thing he wanted, to have to take time off on his first day.'

'Just one of those things. I think he was hoping she'd be over this bit before he started work, but they had to delay the op for a week because of staffing problems with flu or something. Whatever, I'm covering for him this afternoon, so we'd better not be busy!'

Did God have a hotline to their conversations? Maddie wondered later as they were rushed off their feet. Apart from the usual run-of-the-mill non-emergencies that were brought in because the weekend was coming and the parents wanted to get the child seen before Monday, there were the real accidents and emergencies, the children who needed their expertise and excellent diagnostic facilities.

One of them was Maddie's niece Sophie, who had fallen off the stage rehearsing for the school play and banged her head on a chair. She was vomiting, her colour was awful and she couldn't see clearly.

'Auntie Maddie?' she said plaintively, clinging to Maddie's hand. 'I feel sick—'

Maddie whipped a bowl under her chin and smoothed back her hair, while her mother, Maddie's sister-in-law, held her hand and looked anguished.

'She'll be all right, Jude,' Maddie said soothingly. 'She's just got a bit of concussion. Happens all the time.'

'It's just so typical! We were going away this weekend—it's Tom's birthday next week, and we were going to celebrate, and now I don't know how to contact him and we'll have to cancel the hotel and—'

'Hey, hey, calm down,' Maddie said gently, hugging her and settling little Sophie down at the same time. 'I'll get Dad to track him down. You just sit here and breathe gently, and I'll get someone to make you a cup of tea while Daniel has a look at her—OK?'

She nodded, her eyes fixed on her daughter, and Maddie went out, picked up the phone at the nurses' station and dialled her parents' number. Her father answered, and she quickly filled him in, leaving him to contact Tom and pass on the news.

'She is all right, I take it?' her father asked calmly.

'Yes, I think so. Looks like straightforward concussion, but we'll keep her in overnight to be on the safe side, I imagine. Tell him not to worry.'

'Will do. And while I've got you, when are you coming to see us?'

'I'll try and find a moment,' Maddie said evasively, guilt prickling at her. Her parents were lovely, but just recently, especially since they'd had yet another grandchild, they'd started looking at their middle daughter thoughtfully, as if they were wondering how best they could marry her off.

As if they didn't have enough grandchildren already, Maddie thought in exasperation as she went back to Judith. Seven at the last count, and that was excluding the two on the way. Of the four children, she was the only one who was single, the only one without children—the only one to have failed.

And not, she thought achingly, because she was unwilling. She just couldn't bring herself to settle for the wrong man, and to date she hadn't met anyone she could respect and love enough to make a life with.

Inexplicably an image of Rob popped into her mind, and her stride faltered. Silly. Of course she wasn't thinking of him like that. It was just that he was on her mind at the moment, with Angel's op and looking at the flat and Angel's revelation about Rob not being her father. It was just coincidence.

Not even she was that silly—was she?

She went back to her sister-in-law, told her and Daniel, who was busy shining lights and teasing Sophie and examining her by subterfuge, that her father was going to contact Tom, and then immersed herself in her work for the rest of the afternoon.

Tom arrived, and then he and Jude went with Sophie to a ward for further observation of Sophie's condition, which looked as though it was nothing more serious than a simple bang on the head, to everyone's great relief.

It was long past three o'clock, and the late shift including Sarian were there to take over and carry on, but Maddie stayed until things were less frantic. Then, without giving herself time to think about what she was doing and why, she went up to Angel's ward and found Rob sprawled in the chair beside his daughter, his hand through the cot sides holding her hand as she slept. A soft snore escaped him, and a huge lump formed in Maddie's throat.

Poor man. So devoted to his daughter, so torn by their tragedy, so racked by guilt.

Angel stirred, shifting restlessly, and his eyes flickered open. For a moment they were blurred and unfocussed, soft in the gentle light of the cubicle, and then they cleared and Maddie wondered if he could see through to her soul.

If so, she thought, there was probably enough there to send him running for cover.

She dredged up a smile, perched carefully on the foot of the bed and glanced at the still-sleeping child. 'How is she?' she asked softly.

'Clingy. She's all right, better, but still clingy. It's not like her. She's never been like this.'

'There are too many changes all at once,' Maddie said comfortingly. 'She'll be all right—especially once you're in the hospital grounds. That will comfort her.'

He nodded, and some of the anxiety left his eyes. 'You're right. I ought to move my stuff in and make up the bed, but I'm so damn tired I'm tempted to stay here for the night. Anything rather than move.'

'I'll help you,' she offered, before her brain could

kick in. 'We could get a take-away so you didn't have to cook, or eat in the canteen, whatever. They can bleep you then if Angel needs you, and you could pop over and see her and come back.'

He looked severely tempted, but then he shook his head. 'You don't want to do that,' he murmured, but he was wrong.

She did. She wanted to very much—just how much she didn't dare to examine. She just hoped it wouldn't be too obvious to him!

CHAPTER FOUR

'THANKS.'

Maddie straightened up and smiled at Rob across the neatly made bed. 'My pleasure,' she said softly. And then, because she felt too aware of him, standing so close, she went over to the sofa and patted a cushion into shape.

'It'll look better with some things in it,' she said, looking round doubtfully and wondering if she had anything in her flat she could spare—a rug, a throw, a plant—

'Maddie, it's not much more than an accommodation address. It doesn't matter.'

She turned towards him and shook her head. 'You're wrong. It does matter. It's where you'll come to recharge your batteries. It needs to be welcoming and homely.'

For a moment she thought she saw yearning flicker in his eyes, but then it was gone, replaced by the steely core that had held him together all this time. 'I'm used to basic. I've been camping out of a suitcase for a lot of the past eighteen months. Trust me, this is bordering on luxury.'

He smiled, a tight, empty smile that was meant to reassure her and did nothing of the sort. 'How about that take-away you talked about? And then I must go and see Angel. I have to tuck her up for the night.'

So they went round the corner and picked up kebabs, then went back to his flat and washed them down with a bottle of fizzy water from the off-licence, then made a cup of coffee to follow. They ate almost in silence. Then, the coffee made from a kettle in the corner, they sat on the institutional furniture, him with his feet on the coffee-table, her with hers tucked under her bottom, and gradually he seemed to relax.

'Thank you for helping,' he said again, and she smiled and shrugged.

'It's nothing,' she said, and it really wasn't anything very much, but it felt monumental in a way, as if he'd allowed her some huge privilege. She almost felt she should thank him.

How curious.

The night was cold, clear as a bell, with frost sparkling on the trees outside in the overspill of light. 'It's going to be a cold one,' she said, and he nodded.

'It's not far to walk, at least. I'll take you home in a moment, then go and see Angel.'

His head dropped back against the cushion, his eyes closed and within moments he was snoring softly. Poor man. He still had to go and tuck Angel up, and it was nearly nine o'clock. She hated to wake him, but she would have to. Not yet, though. For a few minutes she let him sleep and yearned to cradle that weary head against her breast.

And while he slept, she looked around at the few signs of a personal life. There was a paperweight, a lump of rock that Angel had given him, he said. Books, but not many. Some medical, a couple of thrillers, a book on old gardens. And a picture of Angel, the first time she'd seen the little girl's face without bandages, taken before the accident. She was a bridesmaid, her hair braided up and laced with flowers, her eyes sparkling. She looked gorgeous, and

Maddie thought again what a tragedy her little life had been.

He needed to see her. She woke him with a touch of her hand on his shoulder, and he jerked awake, his eyes flying open and staring at her blankly for a moment.

'Time to go and see Angel, or you'll be saying good morning to her instead of goodnight,' Maddie prompted gently.

He stared in disbelief at his watch, then groaned. 'Oh, Lord. I was going to walk you home—I'll call you a taxi—'

'I'll wait. It's not a problem. I can come with you, if you like, or wait here? Or I can walk back on my own. I do it almost every time I'm on a late.'

His brow creased in a furrow. 'You shouldn't. It isn't safe for you to be on these streets alone at night—'

'Rob, I'm fine. Go and see Angel. I'll stay here and wash up.'

He levered himself to his feet and stared down at her, hesitating just a moment longer before snagging a jacket off the back of the sofa and heading for the door. 'I'll be quick. I'll walk you home when I get back.'

She nodded and watched him go, then, humming softly to herself, she cleared away their mugs and glasses to the communal kitchen, threw out the paper wrappers from the kebabs and wiped down the table. It was such a simple, homely task. It chilled her that it meant so much. Was she really such a sad, shrivelled old spinster that clearing up someone's mess made her feel like a real person?

Oh, heavens.

She turned up the heating, settled down in front of the television and tried not to think about Rob and how alone he was and how much his little daughter needed a mother-figure.

That way, she reminded herself, lay madness. Rob's sole concern at the moment was his daughter. Playing house on her own was one thing. Expecting him to join in was quite another.

She would do well to remember that.

'Night, Angel.'

'Night, Daddy,' she murmured sleepily. He straightened, easing his hand away, but her fingers tightened. 'Are you really just next door?' she asked, her eyes opening a crack.

He could see the worry in them still. 'Really,' he assured her. 'Maybe tomorrow, if it's warm enough, I'll take you over there and you can see it. It's nothing special, but at least I'll be close to you.'

'Did you put my picture up?' she asked.

He nodded. 'Yes, of course. It was the first thing I did.'

'Good.' Her eyes slid shut again. 'Night,' she mumbled.

'Night, my pretty little Angel. Sleep tight.' He bent forwards and kissed her eyes, one at a time, and the tip of her nose. It was all he could reach through the bandages, and it wasn't enough. He pressed her fingers to his lips and squeezed them gently, and she squeezed back, a slow, sleepy squeeze.

He left her then, her breathing deep and even, her eyes shut fast, and headed back to the flat. Would Maddie still be there? He'd been much longer than he'd meant to be, and he had a sudden flicker of fear that she might have walked home alone. If anything had happened to her—

He strode out, his legs eating up the corridors, and palmed the door out of the way, scrunching across the gravel to the flats and stabbing in the code with impatient fingers. If she'd gone—

She was there, curled up in front of the television, the news burbling gently in the background as she slept peacefully in a corner of the sofa. He sighed with relief, went into the bathroom to fill the kettle and then sat down opposite her while he waited for it to boil.

What was it about her presence that made the place seem like a home? Just coming in to find her there did something strange to him, melted a frozen corner of his heart and made him feel, just for the briefest second, that he was glad to be alive.

Not that she would be interested in him, of course. A bitter, lonely widower with a scarred, crippled child and a legacy of pain that sometimes seemed to swamp him—what did he have to offer her? Any woman, come to that, but particularly such a lovely, warm, compassionate woman who could have anyone she chose.

She'd make someone a wonderful wife one day.

Just not him, not ever, because it was a road he'd never dare go down again.

Getting abruptly to his feet, he leant forwards and shook her shoulder. 'Maddie? Wake up.' Wake up and go home, before I forget all my resolutions and let myself fall for those wonderful green-gold eyes and that soft, full mouth and the generous curves of your body—

*　　*　　*

Maddie opened her eyes, startled.

'Rob?' she murmured. She straightened, blinking, and met his eyes. They looked—poleaxed. No. They were just tired. He turned away, heading for the kettle in the corner.

'Coffee?' he said over his shoulder.

'Have you got tea?' She slid her feet to the floor, winced at the pins and needles in her hand and stood up, rotating her wrist carefully. 'I don't usually drink coffee this late at night.'

'Tea has as much caffeine—'

'Not the way I drink it.'

She propped herself against the wall and watched as he made them tea, weak in concession to her caffeine phobia, and then sat down with her hands curled round the mug and blew the steam off the top and wondered what it really had been that she'd seen in his eyes.

'How was Angel?' she asked, changing her mental subject.

'Oh, all right. Better, I think. Less clingy. I think this flat was a good move. I've told her I'll bring her over here tomorrow to see it.'

Maddie nodded. 'If she can visualise you in it she won't feel so cut off. And she'll know it's near.'

'Yes.'

Maddie's mouth dried. She'd run out of platitudes, inane snippets of non-conversation. She swallowed her tea, almost burning herself, and rinsed out her mug in the washbasin.

'Time to go,' she said briskly, and he put down his mug and straightened slowly.

'I'll walk you home.'

'It isn't necessary—'

'It is to me. Humour me, Maddie.'

He helped her into her coat, the same tired old friend she always wore, with the pocket lining frayed from her keys, and then shrugged into his own coat. Pocketing his keys, he flicked off the lights and ushered her out, down the stairs and into the star-studded night. It was cold enough to take her breath away, and she snuggled down inside the collar of her coat and shuddered.

'Chilly, isn't it? Still, it's a beautiful night.'

It was, a truly lovely night and much better than the dark, rainy nights of November. They strode out briskly, their breath fogging in the cold air, and within minutes they turned into her street.

'Thanks, I'll be fine now,' she said, but he took her elbow and escorted her all the way to her front door.

'Now you'll be fine,' he said, smiling wryly. 'Got your keys?'

She pulled them out of her pocket and slipped the red key in the lock. She didn't turn it, though. His voice stopped her, something in it impossible to ignore. Something raw and compelling and linked directly to her soul.

'Maddie?'

That was all, just her name, but she forgot her keys and turned back to him, seeing the loneliness and need in his eyes.

'Thank you for tonight,' he said again.

'My pleasure.'

Afterwards she didn't know which of them had moved first, but his hands were cradling her face, cold and hard and yet curiously gentle, and his firm, cool lips were against hers in a chaste kiss that made her ache for more.

Then his hands dropped to his sides and he was backing away, his eyes still locked with hers. They were filled with yearning, and found an echo in her heart. She swallowed with difficulty.

His mouth twisted into a little smile. 'Sleep tight. See you Monday.'

'And you. Have a good weekend. I hope Angel likes the flat.'

He waited until she'd let herself in and closed the door behind her, then she heard the scrunch of his shoes on the path as he walked away.

Leaning on the wall in the filtered glow of the outside light, she lifted her fingers to her lips. She could still feel the gentle imprint of his mouth, undemanding and yet somehow intensely powerful in its effect on her.

It was just a friendly kiss, she told herself irritably. You're reading much more into it than was there.

It didn't stop her dreaming, though, later that night as she lay restlessly in her bed and ached for something out of reach...

The flat seemed empty without her. Empty and somehow lonelier than he could have imagined.

It was the contrast, he told himself. She was so warm and friendly and open, and without her there the flat seemed colder.

He lay in the bed she'd helped him make, and tried to remember the last time he'd held a woman as warm, as generous as he knew she would be.

Never.

There had never been anyone like her in his life, either before or since his marriage, and certainly not during it. Maria had been unhappy, as lonely as he was. When they'd turned to each other at all, it had been for comfort, a mutual acceptance that the other was the best they had. All they had.

Even that small comfort seemed years ago, and his body ached for the release of a warm, passionate relationship with a woman like Maddie.

No, correct that. *With Maddie.*

A deep groan dragged itself up from inside him, and he screwed his eyes shut against the thin stream of the street lights from the crack in the too-narrow curtains. He longed for the oblivion of total darkness, for the peace of a good night's sleep.

He longed for Maddie's arms around him, but it wasn't going to happen. He had nothing to offer a woman, either now or in the future, and he had Angel to sort out. He rolled to his side, punched his pillow into shape and wondered yet again if Daniel could be her father.

If so, should he know? Poised on the brink of his future with Sarian, would it be fair to tell him? And did it matter?

He rolled to his back again, staring at the pale ceiling in the overspill from the street lamps. It wouldn't change the way he felt about Angel, he realised. He loved her unreservedly for herself, and her genetic base was irrelevant to him.

But to Daniel? Would it be irrelevant to him? He should know if he was a father.

Rob swallowed hard, suddenly conscious of the damp trails that ran down into his hair. He closed his eyes against the tears—tears of helplessness, frustration, anguish at Angel's endless suffering, at the futile waste of Maria's life.

He didn't cry for himself. He didn't feel he merited

that much sympathy. It was all his fault, and that was a cross he'd bear alone, without comfort. It was no more than he deserved.

Sleep was a long time coming.

'It's nice—can I stay here with you? I could sleep in the bed next to you. I wouldn't be a nuisance.'

Rob cradled Angel in his arms and sat on the bed, hugging her gently and taking great care not to press on her still-sore face. 'I know you wouldn't be a nuisance, darling, but I have to go out sometimes at night and it wouldn't be safe for you here alone. Once we've got our own house and a nanny, it'll be all right, but there isn't room for a nanny here.'

'But when you don't have to work—can I stay then?'

He squeezed her gently. 'Maybe. I'll ask the ward sister. She'll know. You have to stay in the ward most of the time until your face has healed completely, to make sure the scars are as fine as possible. We don't want to mess it up.'

She seemed to withdraw a little. 'No,' she said thoughtfully, and, slipping off his lap, she wandered across the room and picked up the picture of her as a bridesmaid. She looked at it for ages, then without a word she set it down and turned back to him. 'Can we go back?' she asked.

He blinked, surprised that she was now suddenly in a hurry to return to the ward. 'Sure.' He stood up, lifted her carefully into his arms and carried her out, back across the gravel path to the hospital and up to her ward.

To his surprise Daniel was there, looking for him, and when he saw them he crouched down and held his arms out. 'Angel, my favourite lady! I thought you'd run away!'

She giggled and hugged him. 'I went to see Daddy's flat. He's going to ask if I can stay there.'

'Maybe sometimes, and not yet, sweetheart. We'll have to talk to the doctors and nurses,' Rob reminded her.

Daniel perched one lean hip on the end of the bed. 'I'm running errands, actually. I've got a car full of stuff for you from Maddie—where do you want it?'

'Stuff?'

'A plant, a rug, a couple of cushions. She said your flat needed some warmth.'

It did—but it needed Maddie's warmth. Still, her gifts were the next best thing. 'Where are you parked?' he asked.

'Under the hospital, in my slot. Don't worry, I'm not in a hurry. The girls have gone shopping for wedding things.'

'Wedding things?' Angel said, peering up at him, and Daniel floundered for a second, their secret nearly out.

'Yeah. They're going to a wedding—they need clothes.'

Angel's eyes were suddenly liquid, and she turned away. 'I've got a new colouring book. I want to do it.' She hopped up on the bed, pulled the book off her locker and unzipped her crayons, then started studiously filling in the outline of a fairy.

Too studiously. Why? Did she miss shopping with her mother? Life was a minefield, Rob thought with a quiet sigh. 'Are you all right, poppet?' he asked gently.

'Uh-huh. I'm colouring.'

'I can see that. It's good. I like that fairy. Can I go with Daniel and put these things in my flat, then come back?'

'Yup,' she said, her face behind its mask hidden to him, expressionless. It was so hard to work out what she was thinking.

He stood up. 'Shall we?'

They left her to it, unaware of the huge, heavy tears that soaked out of her eyes and drenched the wool and crêpe that covered her cheeks.

'Thank you for the bits and pieces.'

Maddie looked up with a smile, pleased to see that he appeared less exhausted than he had before the weekend. 'My pleasure. I hope you didn't think I was interfering.'

His mouth twitched into a slight smile. 'Not at all. It looks much better, you were right.'

A little glow of happiness spread through her. 'Thanks,' she said softly. She'd been so worried he'd take offence.

He looked at the white-board she was writing on, studying the names and details. 'How did you get on with your wedding shopping?' he asked under his breath, scanning down the list.

Maddie looked around to make sure they were alone. 'Fruitless. Sarian doesn't know what she wants—just what she doesn't want!'

He chuckled. 'I know the feeling. I hate shopping. Should I take a look at this lad in Cubicle Three?'

'Ben? He's a regular. He skateboards in competitions, and he often gets smashed up at the weekend and doesn't tell his parents, and then on Monday morning he can hardly move and comes in with Mum.

This time it looks like he's actually broken something.'

'Ribs,' Rob said, nodding at the list. 'OK. Notes on the clip outside?'

'Yes.' She led him to the cubicle, but there were no notes on the clip. Instead Ben was sitting up on the couch reading them. Maddie removed them gently but firmly, and he gave her a cock-eyed grin.

'That was just getting interesting,' he complained.

'Cheeky monkey,' she said affectionately. 'Where's Mum?'

'Gone to the loo.'

Rob grinned and leant back against the desk, arms folded. 'So, what's the diagnosis, Doctor?'

Ben looked sheepish. 'Dunno. My ribs hurt something chronic.'

'Might have a flail chest, eh, Sister?'

'Could be, Doctor—or a pneumothorax. Perhaps we need to do a thoracotomy?'

The boy's eyes widened. 'No way!' he said, clutching his chest defensively. 'It's not that bad!'

'Watch a lot of that sort of stuff on the telly, do you?' Rob asked, eyeing him curiously.

'Yeah—when it's on. I want to be a doctor when I grow up.'

'If you live that long,' his mother said drily coming into the cubicle. 'Sometimes I wonder. Hello, Maddie. Hello, Doctor.'

Rob held his hand out. 'Robert Oliver. So, can you tell me what happened and how?'

'Missed a jump,' he said dourly. 'Lost my board at the top of the slope and crashed on the ramp. Stupid. I can do it much better, but I was pushing myself. I was winning till that happened,' he added morosely.

'Why don't you take up something safe, like sky-diving?' Rob said mildly, prodding with caution at the black and blue ribs in front of him.

'Ouch. Don't be sarky. I love skateboarding, and I'm good at it.'

'So I gather. You won't be doing it for a while, though, I don't think. These ribs are almost certainly broken. We need a few pictures of that, and then we can decide what to do.'

They were broken, but not badly enough to merit surgery or admission. He was strapped up, sent home with painkillers and told to rest.

'Not that he will. He'll be back on that darned thing in days, I bet,' Maddie said with resignation.

Daniel stuck his head round the door. 'Rob? The ward want a word with you—Angel's been crying, apparently.'

'Oh, hell.' He glanced at his watch, looked at Maddie and sighed. 'I'll ring them. I don't have time to go up there, there's a queue of patients needing my attention.'

She looked at him, at the concern in his eyes, the worry nagging at him, and told him to go. 'There's a lot we can do without you, and it will give Daniel something to do. He mustn't get complacent now Tim's retiring and he's a consultant!'

Rob threw her the vestige of a smile and left. Maddie went to find Daniel, just on his way into a cubicle. 'I've sent him off to the ward,' she said, and he nodded.

'He worries.'

'He needs to. She's a very sad little girl.'

Maddie eyed Daniel thoughtfully. She'd known him for ages. Could she ask him about Maria? Could she interfere and ask if there was any chance that Angel was his child?

Then Sarian came out of the cubicle, her eyes softening as she looked at Daniel, and Maddie knew she couldn't do anything to upset the smooth and even course of their romance.

'Problems?' Sarian said, looked across at Maddie.

'Angel's upset. Rob's gone to see her.'

Sarian nodded. 'Good. Daniel, I think this lad will need investigating. Would you look at him?'

'Sure.' He threw Maddie a grin. 'Let me know when he comes back down.'

She nodded and turned away, getting back to the queue of patients and hoping that nothing urgent cropped up while Rob was off the unit. She didn't want to have to call him back.

'Talk to me, darling.'

Angel sniffed and snuggled closer. 'I just missed you,' she mumbled wetly.

Peggie O'Neill paused beside them and smiled gently. 'Hi, Angel. How're you doing, poppet?'

'She's a bit down at the moment,' Rob told the young doctor.

'Down? We can't have that! Everyone has to be happy up here—I tell you what, why don't you and I see if we can find something nice for you to do? I think some of the children are painting this morning—do you think you could join in? Are you feeling well enough?'

Angel nodded half-heartedly, and Peggie held out

her hand. 'Come on, then. We'll go and find the others.'

Rob followed them down the ward to the playroom, a hive of industry as usual. He glanced worriedly at his watch. Maybe this would distract Angel enough so that he could go back to work, because one thing was sure, being here with her wasn't helping either, and he had a host of children down in A and E who also needed him.

'Oh, look, a wedding!' Peggie exclaimed with a smile.

The child looked up from her painting. It was Cara, the little girl who'd had the scrape in the playground, and she smiled at Peggie through her bandages. 'It's you and Mr Davies,' Cara told her.

'Are you getting married?' Angel asked.

'Yes,' Peggie told her with a broad smile. 'We are—in twelve days' time—just after your stitches come out.'

'Will you have bridesmaids?' Angel asked, and Rob thought he could hear a catch in her voice.

'Yes, two—my cousins.'

'What are they wearing?' Cara asked. 'I have to paint them.'

'Oh, pale blue,' Peggie said with a smile.

'I was a bridesmaid,' Angel said, and Rob remembered the picture in his flat. That was the wedding of one of her Portuguese cousins, a big, flashy affair with lots of little girls running around with flowers in their hair and frothy dresses and tinkling laughter.

They'd been gorgeous, and remembering it brought a lump to his throat. She'd been so pretty. So perfect.

Damn.

Peggie left them, and Angel settled down next to Cara and started painting.

'Sweetheart, I have to go back to work for a while,' he said cautiously, anticipating a protest, but there was none.

'OK. See you later,' she said, dipping her brush into a pot of white paint and sloshing it on the paper. Unless he missed his guess it was going to be another wedding picture, probably with hundreds of bridesmaids and bright splodgy flowers and shocking pink skin.

He stifled a smile, kissed her on the top of her head and left her with Cara. She seemed happy enough. He'd get back to work quick while the going was good.

He went back down to the A and E unit, and threw himself back into the fray. It was almost one before they paused for breath.

'Perfect timing,' a voice said, and Maureen Chappell, the senior A and E sister, joined the group standing by the nurses' station. 'I'm selling tickets for the Friends of Lizzie's Ball the week after next. Any takers?'

Daniel suddenly looked a little awkward—no, not awkward, more wary, Rob thought. 'I'll have two,' he said, reaching for his wallet.

'So that's you and Maddie—I might have known you would, you always go to these things together. Sarian? How about you? And Rob?'

'We could make up a foursome,' Daniel said quickly, covering the awkward pause without giving the game away. 'Here, I'll pay for them all. They can pay me back later.'

Sister Chappell moved on, happy with her success, and Maddie gave Daniel and Sarian a relieved smile.

'Well done. What are you going to do with the other two tickets, now Annie's stolen my escort?'

Sarian looked stunned, but Maddie hugged her briefly. 'Don't look like that. Daniel and I are and only ever have been good friends. We just like going out to the same things, and it helps fend the women off. But this time, I don't think it'll be necessary, so I'll pass.'

Daniel looked from her to Rob and back.

'Rob'll take you,' he said, and the words hung in the air.

He should say something, Rob thought, but the very idea of taking her to a ball brought such vivid images to mind that they took his breath away. Holding her, sliding his arms around her waist, feeling her body sway against his—

'I don't think he fancies the idea,' Maddie said lightly, and he looked up, into soft, wounded green eyes shot through with liquid gold. They shimmered, and in that instant he knew he'd never wanted anything as much as he wanted to take Maddie to that ball.

'Wrong,' he corrected, fishing for his wallet. 'How much is it for two tickets?'

He wrote a cheque, snapped it out of his chequebook with a flourish and handed it to Daniel, taking a pair of tickets in exchange. He tucked them in his wallet and looked across at Maddie.

'So, Cinderella, you *shall* go to the ball,' he murmured, and wondered if she felt one tiny fraction of the anticipation that ripped through him at the thought.

CHAPTER FIVE

'SO, WHEN'S the great day going to be?' Maddie asked Sarian in a quiet moment at the end of her shift.

She shrugged. 'I don't know. We haven't really decided. Soon—but Daniel doesn't seem to be able to decide what he wants.'

Maddie chuckled. 'A bit like you and the dress.'

'It's hard to choose a dress for an unknown venue,' Sarian said drily, then added diffidently, 'Anyway, I can't get used to clothes looking good on me.'

'Well, it's time you did,' Maddie told her firmly. 'You're gorgeous, Annie. I think you have to sort out the venue and make some firm arrangements, then choose something appropriate for that occasion. Whatever, I think you probably want simple, don't you? I don't see you in loads of fussy stuff.'

Sarian laughed. 'Thank goodness we're agreed on that.' Then her smile faded. 'I just wish we had time to sit down and talk it out.'

'So what do you want?' Maddie asked. 'Let me guess—quiet, unfussy, no pomp and ceremony, not too many people—right so far?'

Sarian gave a wry grin. 'You've known me too long,' she said.

'So tell him what *you* want, and see if he agrees. At least it'll start you talking about it.'

'If we ever find time. We seem to have been so busy—one of us is always at work, and when we're not...'

Sarian looked thoughtful, and Maddie wondered how good Daniel was at talking about things. In all the time she'd known him he'd hardly ever said anything that could be construed as remotely private. Obviously he was different with Sarian, but she sensed that there was still something of himself that he held back. Time would sort it out, but he'd been alone too long for an instant adjustment.

She thought of Rob and how he dealt alone with all his mountainous worries. And how many people had the slightest idea how lonely and empty *her* life was? None. Not even Annie, unless she simply guessed.

She dragged her mind off her self-pitying kick and back to the subject of the wedding plans. Maybe if she got them together and they all sat down and talked—

She stood up, rinsed out her mug and dried it, then looked at Sarian still propped up in the corner cuddling her tea. 'I'm going shopping—I've got no food in the house, and I thought I might do a meal for all of us tonight—unless you've got other plans?'

Sarian shook her head. 'Not as far as I know. Check with Daniel, but that sounds lovely. Are you including Rob?'

'Is she including Rob in what?' Rob asked, coming into the staff room and making Maddie jump.

'Supper,' she said, wondering if the warmth she felt in her cheeks was visible or just a figment of her imagination. 'I thought I'd cook for us all, if anyone's interested.'

'Put me down on the list,' Daniel said with a grin, following him in. 'I'm starving. OK, Sarian? You game?'

'Suits me.'

Daniel reached for a couple of mugs. 'Are you doing a casserole?' he asked hopefully.

'Chicken marengo?'

'Excellent. Rob, are you coming?'

Maddie held her breath, unwilling to admit that without him the evening, for her at least, would fall flat.

'If you're sure—?'

Her breath eased out in a silent sigh. 'Of course I'm sure. When are you all off?'

Sarian wrinkled her nose. 'I'm on a late. I won't be in till after nine.'

'That's what you get for having a lie-in,' Maddie said virtuously. 'I was up at six—but don't worry, we'll wait for you.'

'I'll hang on here at the hospital and walk you back,' Daniel offered, then turned to Rob. 'I could kill time in your flat, if you don't mind? Will you be there?'

'Some of the time. I have to see Angel, of course, but you're welcome to use it whether I'm there or not.'

Maddie dusted off her hands, pulled off her tabard and shook her hair loose. 'Right. I'll see you all for supper just after nine, then. Don't be late, or I'll eat it all,' she warned.

A chorus of cheeky comments followed her down the corridor, and she chucked her tabard in the laundry bin, pulled on her coat and headed for the shops. No doubt the shopping would pull her fingers off as usual, but the thought of Rob coming for supper made her hum as she hurried along the busy streets.

Suddenly life didn't seem so bleak and empty after all.

*   *   *

'Well, Maddie got out in the nick of time. I wonder if she knew what was coming?' Daniel said drily as they prepared Resus for an influx.

Rob gave a grunt of laughter. 'Wise woman,' he muttered, scanning the room for things they might need. A school minibus on its way to a swimming gala had been involved in an accident, and several of the children had been hurt. Until they arrived there was no way of knowing how badly hurt they were, but they knew at least two were trapped and being cut free, and it was those two they were most concerned about.

The first of the approaching sirens had them going to the door of the ambulance bay to check the arrivals, and it was soon evident that most of them had shock and the odd bruise. Still, minor fractures and internal injuries couldn't be ruled out, and for a while they were all working at full stretch.

Then one of the trapped children was brought in, and she had a nasty injury to her right leg. There were several fractures, a great deal of soft tissue damage and Rob thought it quite possible she'd lose it.

What a tragedy. Still, their first priority was to stabilise her for theatre. He was working with Maureen Chappell, brisk, efficient and highly competent, and together they took blood for cross matching, checked her for other signs of injury and talked to her.

She was crying softly, her pain only blurred at the edges by the medication, and Rob could only guess what she was going through. He wished again that Maddie was here to talk to her, but to his astonishment Maureen, so stern and unapproachable, was kindness itself with the little girl.

'OK, she's stable now,' Rob said, checking her vi-

tal signs yet again. They'd given her intravenous flu-
ids to stop the pressure drop, and he was satisfied now
that she was ready for theatre. 'Can we have some
pictures, please? Chest, spine and legs for starters.
Where's the orthopaedic reg?'

The mobile X-ray was moved into place, and the
moment the plates were developed one of the orthopaedic team came in. 'Sorry for the delay, I was in
theatre. They're clearing up and standing by. What
have we got?' she said, and quickly scanned the
plates. 'Some of these ribs have cracked—nothing
displaced. That leg's a doozy. OK, we'll take her now
and sort her out. I think soft tissue's going to be a
priority. That blood supply looks a bit iffy. Can I have
another X-ray of the leg from this side? Send it up to
theatre after her, please. We'll make a start. Do we
have consent?'

'Her parents are being contacted. The teacher said
they're having difficulty finding them, but they'd
signed a consent form giving permission for any necessary treatment—standard procedure for a school
trip,' Maureen told her. 'I would take it as a given.
I'll get the parents to sign the minute they come in.'

The orthopaedic registrar nodded. 'OK. I'll go and
scrub again. Can you send her up when the plate's
done?'

The moment the X-ray was taken, the girl was
whisked away to theatre, and Rob stripped off his
blood-stained gloves and gown and threw them in the
bin.

'How're you doing, sport?' Daniel asked, coming
up behind him.

'OK. What about the others?'

'All sorted, nothing major. We're off duty. Shall we go?'

Rob shot Daniel a quick look, but his face was blank. Odd. He had the distinct feeling his friend was as taut as a bowstring, but there was no outward sign of it.

'Sure,' he agreed, and minutes later they were sitting down in his flat with a cup of tea and a packet of biscuits.

At least, Rob was sitting down. Daniel was prowling, fingering things, picking them up and putting them down, shifting restlessly around the room like a caged tiger.

'What is it, Easy?' he asked quietly. Surely to God he wasn't about to tell him he was Angel's father—

'I don't know what to do about the wedding.'

Rob felt his shoulders drop with relief. He was getting paranoid. 'What about it?' he asked. Then he straightened, another possibility occurring to him. 'You aren't having second thoughts?'

Daniel laughed and shook his head. 'Oh, no. Nothing like that. Sarian's the best thing that's ever happened to me. I love her so much it hurts. No— it's the ceremony. I feel a bit schizophrenic about it. Part of me wants a nice, simple, civil marriage—and another part I thought I'd buried long ago is telling me I won't be married unless I'm married in the eyes of God.'

He stabbed his fingers through his hair, rumpling the fair strands and leaving them in disarray. He stopped at the window, staring sightlessly out over the grounds. The lights were on along the pathway, but he didn't seem to see them.

Was he seeing his father? The man had been fanatically religious, and from what he'd gleaned over the years Rob understood Daniel's childhood to have been strict to the point of cruelty. Not just physical cruelty—he'd seen the evidence of that—but a deeper, more insidious persecution. Yet obviously some of that doctrine had stuck—enough to make his friend uncertain about a civil ceremony, at least.

'Why not get married in the hospital chapel?' he suggested cautiously. 'I passed it yesterday with Angel, and the chaplain stopped for a chat. You must have met him. He seemed really pleasant and friendly, wonderful with Angel, and the chapel was just very simple—an ideal setting, I would have thought. You could explain—'

'Explain what?' Daniel said tightly. 'That my father beat me? That if I hear a hymn or a prayer I feel sick inside?'

'Yes—if that's what it takes. Easy, it was a long time ago. You're not the defenceless child you were then. Your father was ill. You have to forgive him— or at least move on. You have to let go of the past to make the best of your future. Maybe now's the time.'

Daniel straightened, peering down into the pools of light along the path. 'Do you believe in fate?' he murmured.

'Fate?'

'Mmm.'

Rob watched as his friend paused, then headed for the door, looking grimly determined. 'Back in a bit.'

The door banged, and Rob could hear footsteps running down the stairs and then the crunch of gravel. He watched from the window as Daniel sprinted towards the hospital, reaching the door at the same time as another man he recognized as the chaplain.

They paused, exchanging a few words, and then the man laid his hand on Daniel's shoulder and ushered him into the hospital and out of sight.

Hopefully the chaplain would be able to lay the ghost in Daniel's past.

The doorbell rang on the stroke of nine o'clock, and Maddie gave her hands a quick swipe with her apron as she untied it, cast a despairing glance at her glowing complexion and untidy hair, and pulled the door open.

It was Rob, bearing a bottle of wine and a small bunch of flowers. 'Nothing special—I got them from the hospital shop, I'm afraid,' he said with a rueful smile.

Maddie was glad she was already flushed, because she felt herself glow warmer. 'Thank you,' she said, touched and pleased that he had bothered. 'They're lovely. I'll find a vase. Come in.'

He hung his coat on the hook on the back of the door, and she could feel the cold coming off it. Maybe she'd go and stand outside and let the night air cool her cheeks.

'Come on through to the kitchen. I'm sort of done, but I was just laying the table. The others aren't here yet.'

'I'll give you a hand,' he said easily, trailing her down the corridor and making her wonder if the loose-cut trousers she was wearing really were flattering or if she looked like a house from the back. She sucked in her bottom and stood up straighter.

'Have a seat,' she said, snatching out a chair and all but pushing him into it. 'If I give you stuff you can lay the table, but there isn't room in here for us both to wander round.'

And that way, she thought, I won't be bumping into you every ten seconds.

She stifled the pang of regret, dumped a handful of cutlery on the table and turned her attention back to the stove. The potatoes were done, so she drained them and left them to steam for a moment before mashing them. The chicken was catching slightly on the bottom—it always caught on the bottom, and she had to remember to stir it occasionally or it would burn. She prodded it with a fork and decided it was cooked enough.

Rob paused in his table-laying to sniff appreciatively. 'Smells good,' he murmured.

'Thanks.' She pushed it to the back of the hob for a moment, passed him a corkscrew and a handful of glasses, and put the wine he'd brought in front of him.

'Let's have a drink,' she suggested, and almost jumped when his fingers closed over the neck of the bottle and brushed hers.

She turned back to the stove, wondering if the light touch of his hand had been deliberate or if she was just reading things into it that didn't exist.

Probably. Why would he be interested in her? She was everybody's mother. She always had been. Men didn't want mothering, they wanted clever little sex symbols that knew all the moves and didn't ask for anything in return.

Not emotional women that got clingy and demanding and assumed a commitment that wasn't there—

'Something I did?' Rob said softly, his hands coming to rest on her shoulders.

She stiffened. 'What?'

'You're beating the living daylights out of that mashed potato. I just wondered if it was my fault.'

Her shoulders dropped, and she let her head fall forwards and gave a strangled laugh. 'No. Nothing you've done. I was just thinking about someone else.'

'Ouch. Will you ever see them again?'

She shook her head. 'Him—and no, I won't.'

'That might be just as well, unless you're into prison food. I wouldn't fancy his chances.'

She put the masher down and turned to face him. His hands had fallen away, but came back to cup her arms gently. 'Want to talk about it?' he asked.

She shook her head again and smiled. 'No. It was over years ago.' Too many years. She'd been on the shelf so long now the dust was inches thick. Ah, well. 'How about that drink?'

'It's poured.'

He turned and scooped up the glasses, pressing one into her hand. 'Here's to the future,' he said with a ghost of a smile playing around his lips, and she laughed softly and raised her glass, clinking it against his.

'To the future,' she murmured, and wondered what it would hold.

More of the same?

Or something else? Something warm and wonderful and permanent, with a man who made her heart beat faster and her knees go weak at the thought of him?

She took a gulp of wine, set the glass down and turned hastily back to the stove before he could see the longing in her eyes.

'Anything I can do?'

'No, it's all done now,' she said, realising that it

was and there was nothing left for her to distract herself with. She picked up her glass and sat down at the table, turning sideways in the chair so her back was against the wall and her feet were up on the other chair. That way she didn't have to look at him unless she chose to—which she didn't.

Just now she was convinced her face was an open book, and she needed time to school her expression before she let him read her. She was feeling stunned, shocked by the realisation that, for her at least, this relationship could easily lead to more. Much, much more—

'I wonder where the others are?' Rob said after a second.

Maddie glanced at her watch and shrugged. 'Sometimes you have to finish a case—you can't just escape. That's why I do things that can keep hot. Everything's ready now. I'll just throw boiling water on the frozen peas when they arrive.'

Rob nodded, then trailed one lean, blunt-tipped finger round the top of his glass. It squeaked, and he dipped his finger in the wine and tried again, making the glass sing. It went right through her, tangling with her ragged nerves.

'So, how's the flat?' she asked brightly.

'Oh, fine. Thanks for the bits. It makes it much more homely—you ought to come and look.'

She smiled slightly. She'd been dying to look, but she'd been waiting for an invitation. And now she had it, she wasn't sure she dared to take him up on it! She'd probably make a total fool of herself, and how she was going to get through the charity ball without going gaga she had not the slightest idea. If he so much as touched her—

The doorbell split the silence like an axe, and it was only with the most enormous self-control that she managed not to run to let Daniel and Sarian in. Instead she managed a dignified walk, head up, heart pounding, and opened the door to them with what she hoped was a smile.

They probably wouldn't have noticed if she'd got a bag over her head, she thought drily. They were so wrapped up in each other they were almost oblivious to the rest of the world.

Well, not quite. Daniel dropped a kiss on her cheek, pressed a bottle of wine into her hand and Sarian gave her a box of truffles. 'For later,' she said with a grin. 'Unless we've been so long you've eaten?'

'No, of course not. It was an idle threat, as you well know. Come on in. Rob's here.'

He was, standing in the kitchen where before he'd been sitting, and suddenly the small room seemed full of bodies. Well, full of Rob's, at least. It was only his she was aware of.

She boiled the kettle and scalded the peas while they fussed around and got drinks and settled down in their chairs, then she dished up on the side because there wasn't room on the table, and handed them their plates.

'Wow, smells fantastic,' Rob said, almost inhaling it. Maddie sat down opposite him—the only chair left—and threw him a smile.

'Thanks. It's dead easy—that's why I do it.'

'She's a brilliant cook,' Daniel chipped in. 'Makes the best shortbread—and her buckwheat salad is out of this world.'

'It's the dressing—I buy it in a jar ready-made. It's such a cheat,' she told him, embarrassed by Daniel's praise. 'Anyway,' she added, attacking her chicken, 'enough of me, what about this wedding? Any thoughts yet?'

There was a sudden silence, and she thought, Oh-oh, I've done it again, but when she looked up they were looking into each other's eyes and smiling lovingly.

'It's all settled,' Daniel said, his voice a little gruff. 'We're getting married at nine o'clock on Saturday week in the hospital chapel. We'd like you two to be witnesses.'

She set her fork down, looked across at Sarian for confirmation and found it in the love she saw shining in her old friend's eyes.

'Saturday week?' she said, suddenly focussing. 'That's quick. You aren't—um—?'

'No, I'm not um,' Sarian said with a little smile. 'We just don't see the point in waiting. We want to be married.'

Six hours ago Annie had been in despair. Now it was sorted—and without Maddie's chicken marengo to act as ombudsman! Oh, well. She speared a mushroom on her fork and grinned. 'That's excellent. Right, Annie, we'd better go shopping again. The shops are open late with Christmas coming up, so if we can manage a day when we're both on an early, maybe we'll be able to sort you out.'

'Typical,' Daniel said fondly. 'Any excuse for a shopping trip.'

'Daniel, it's her *wedding* day!' Maddie spluttered, and then caught his grin. 'Eat up,' she growled, 'or you won't get pudding.'

No chance. Both men polished off two generous helpings of the casserole, then groaned in delight when she produced a warm apple crumble from the oven, and fresh, thick cream to pour over it.

'My cholesterol level just doubled,' Rob said, pushing the bowl away and shaking his head to more. 'That was fantastic, Maddie. I don't suppose you fancy a job?'

'Feeding you?' She laughed, crushing the thought that nothing would make her happier. 'Don't be idle. Walk to the canteen if you don't want to cook. I have a life.'

Something died in his eyes, and she could have kicked herself. She didn't mean it like that, and anyway, she didn't have a life. Just an existence.

'I'll do it part-time in exchange for borrowing your muscles periodically,' she said in conciliation, and he arched a brow enquiringly.

'My muscles?' he murmured, and Maddie felt heat rush to her cheeks.

'Muscles,' she confirmed. 'To move things and lug bags of compost for the garden and put the bins out—difficult stuff like that. Man stuff.'

He nodded. 'Sounds like a deal. Want anything moved tonight? I could do with a workout!' He smiled, and the awkward moment was gone.

The party broke up before midnight, because everyone was on duty early the next day. Rob went back to his flat, and Daniel and Sarian sent her out into the sitting room to put her feet up while they washed up.

There was a lot of giggling and splashing, and Maddie lay her head back against the sofa and tried not to feel left out. She was thrilled for them both. Delighted.

So why did it hurt so much?

*   *   *

Angel seemed to be progressing well, and the following day Rob asked Maddie up to his flat after work to see how it looked, and Angel was there. She gave Maddie a stiff little smile through her bandages, and Maddie grinned back and dropped into the seat opposite her.

'How are you?' she asked. 'More comfy?'

Angel nodded solemnly. 'Yes, thank you. I have my bandages off in a week and one day.'

'I bet you're really looking forward to that,' Maddie said, wrinkling her nose. 'It must be horrid being all tied up. Still, at least it's not hot at the moment.'

Angel nodded and turned back to the television in the corner, and Rob sat down next to her and hugged her, and shot Maddie a smile. 'So, what do you think of the flat?' he asked.

She looked around, noticing her plant was surviving and the rug made a focal point of the seating area. The cushions did something extra for the seating, as well. She snuggled back into her chair and smiled.

'Good. I like it. It's getting better.'

He glanced at his watch. 'Look, we were going to have a take-away—do you fancy joining us? There's a southern-fried chicken place down the road, or we could have Chinese—'

'Not Chinese!' Angel wailed, and he threw up his hands and laughed.

'OK, not Chinese. Maybe pizza or something.'

Maddie smiled at them both a little tentatively. 'Are you sure? I don't want to be in the way.'

He shook his head, and Angel shrugged. ''S OK, you're not in the way,' she mumbled, eyes on the screen. 'But I want chicken.'

'You know what?' Maddie said, warmed that they wanted her to join them. 'I *love* southern-fried chicken. Especially the finger-licking bit.'

'Me, too,' Angel said, abandoning her television programme for a moment. 'I haven't had it for *ages.*'

'Oh, at least a week,' Rob said with a grin.

'Nearly two.'

'Hmm. So, Maddie, would you be a love and stay with Angel for a moment while I slip round the corner? I don't like to leave her and there's no point in us all going out in the cold.'

'Of course not,' Maddie agreed with a smile, and wondered, depressingly, if he'd really wanted her to join them or if he'd just wanted her to babysit while he went out.

'He was going to take me in the car,' Angel said as the door closed behind him, 'but I didn't want to miss the television. I'm glad you're here so I didn't have to.'

Maddie smiled slightly at her and watched as she again became riveted to the screen. It was a trailer for a film, and it showed a little bridesmaid running riot at a wedding. Maddie chuckled, but then noticed that Angel looked away, found the remote control and changed channels.

Significant?

'There's a picture of you as a bridesmaid on the cupboard, isn't there?' she said tentatively.

Angel stiffened, then nodded. 'Yes. It's old. I don't look like that any more.'

Oh, Lord, a minefield. Was this what had been upsetting her recently? 'No, I expect you're different,' Maddie said with caution. 'You're quite a bit older now. People change as they get older. Of course I can't tell because of the bandages. I'm looking forward to seeing the real you.'

Angel turned and looked at her, her soft brown eyes wide and vulnerable. Maddie smiled encouragingly, but Angel didn't respond.

'I'm going to be pretty again,' she said firmly. 'Mr Davies said so, and so did Peggie. Then I can be a bridesmaid again, maybe.'

Maddie was cut to the quick by the child's simple statement. 'What do you mean, then you can be a bridesmaid again?'

'I was going to be a bridesmaid for my cousin, but after the accident she said she didn't want me. Daddy said it was because I was ill and upset, but I know it was because I've got a limp and I'm not pretty.'

Oh, heavens, she was going to cry. She blinked hard. Angel needed her help, not her pity. 'Darling, I'm sure your daddy was right,' she said gently. 'I expect they were just thinking of you. If it was my wedding, I wouldn't worry what you looked like or if you were in a wheelchair. I'd want you anyway.'

Angel stared at her with wide eyes for a moment, then said hopefully, 'Are you getting married?'

Maddie shook her head regretfully, and saw Angel's face fall, even with the bandages. 'Unfortunately not—but if I do, would you be my bridesmaid? There'd be lots of you, because I've got lots of nieces and nephews, but if you wouldn't mind joining in it would be lovely.'

Angel's eyes seemed to fill, and she turned away. 'That would be cool,' she said, but her little voice cracked just a fraction.

It was too much for Maddie. She crossed to the settee, scooped Angel up in her arms and hugged her hard. 'My pleasure, sweetheart.' She put her down and smoothed her tangled hair back off her bandages. 'Now, do you think it would be a good idea to get some plates and cutlery?'

Angel shook her head. 'No. We eat it with our fingers and the drinks are in paper cups. It's easy like that. Then we don't have to fight over the washing-up.'

Maddie laughed and stood up. 'OK, then. Sounds good to me.' She heard footsteps on the stairs, and then a tap, and opened the door to find Rob laden down with bags and buckets of goodies.

'Thanks,' he said, throwing her a smile, and despite the cold he brought in with him she felt warm all the way to her toes.

It was a lovely evening. They ate far too much, she and Angel giggled outrageously and made Rob pretend to be cross, and then finally he took Angel back to her ward with a promise to Maddie not to be too long, and walked Maddie home.

On the way she told him about her conversation with Angel. 'Do you suppose that could be why she's been upset?' she asked.

He nodded thoughtfully. 'Of course! Every time she's looked sad, there's been something about a wedding, either on the television, or everyone on the ward talking about Peggie and Gareth's wedding.'

Maddie paused on the doorstep and turned to Rob. 'I don't suppose—?'

'Just what I was thinking,' he murmured. 'Let's ask them.'

CHAPTER SIX

'A BRIDESMAID?' Sarian said thoughtfully. 'Maddie, I'd love to have you as a bridesmaid, but I didn't think you'd want—'

'Not me, silly,' Maddie said with a laugh. 'Angel.'

'Angel?' Daniel murmured. 'What a wonderful idea! Will her bandages be off? She'd hate to have them on for photos.'

'What photos?' Sarian said, alarmed.

'The photos I'll be taking,' Maddie told her firmly, 'so that your children and grandchildren have something to laugh about.'

'Yes, they will be off,' Rob put in, dragging them back to the topic. 'Please, if you don't like the idea, do say no, but she just seems to have got this thing that nobody wants her because of her scars and her limp.'

Sarian's grey eyes softened to pools of mist. 'Oh, poor, precious child—of course we don't mind! We'd love to have her,' she said firmly.

Of course she would say yes, Maddie thought. After all the teasing and snide remarks Annie had endured as a fat, spotty teenager, she would understand Angel's fears.

'There *is* the question of secrecy,' Maddie pointed out. 'If you don't want to tell anyone about the wedding until afterwards, to save fuss, might it be difficult to get Angel to keep such an exciting secret—?'

'No way,' Rob and Daniel said together, and then laughed.

'She's brilliant at keeping secrets,' Daniel said.

'Too good,' Rob added quietly. 'She won't tell a soul. We could find a place that would let us bring a few dresses home for her to try on in the flat, and on the morning of the wedding she could change there and just slip across from the flats with us and she'd be virtually at the chapel, with no one the wiser.'

'Wonderful,' Sarian said, and looked misty-eyed again. 'Oh, I know I didn't want a lot of pomp, but one little bridesmaid will just be the icing on the cake! I'm thrilled! Thank you for suggesting it.'

Maddie laughed in relief. 'Thank goodness. I've already promised her she can be bridesmaid at my wedding, but as I'm not likely to have one in the foreseeable future, it was a bit of an empty threat. Bless you, Annie. And talking of icing, are you having a cake?'

'Hadn't really thought that far. I don't really think we need one, do we?' She looked doubtfully at Daniel, who shook his head.

'Seems a lot of fuss just for so few of us.'

'I think so,' Sarian agreed. 'Let's just go out for coffee somewhere nice afterwards, and have a sticky cream cake instead for a treat.'

'Steady on,' Maddie said with a laugh. 'A whole cream cake? And what about a honeymoon? You *are* going away for the weekend at least, aren't you?'

Daniel shrugged. 'We thought we'd save the money towards a house. If we're careful we can put a deposit together in a year or two. Anyway, now Rob's in his own flat—' He trailed off and shrugged self-consciously, a tentative smile playing around his mouth. 'We don't really need to go away. We just need time together.'

Maddie caught Rob's eye, and nodded as he jerked his head almost imperceptibly towards the door.

'Right, I'm off to bed,' she announced, standing up. Rob followed suit, and they made their farewells and headed downstairs. At her door, Maddie paused and turned to him with a smile.

'You thinking what I'm thinking?' she said softly.

'That they should have a honeymoon? Absolutely. Want to chip in on the cost of the room? We could book them into the honeymoon suite of a hotel for the night—spoil them a bit.'

Maddie nodded. 'Absolutely. And if you don't mind, I'll come over to your flat and decorate their cake. I'll make it tomorrow, once I've got the ingredients, but they can't not have a cake! They'll need to give some to everyone in the department on Monday, otherwise they'll be slaughtered for keeping it a secret! They'll all be quite cross enough as it is.'

Rob gave a soft chuckle. 'I quite agree. Right, we'll liaise about the cake decorating—and thanks for the help with Angel. You're a star, Maddie.'

He bent forwards and brushed her lips with his, just once, just lightly. Then with a ghost of a smile he walked away, let himself out and shut the door softly behind him, leaving Maddie weak at the knees and wondering if his goodnight kisses would always be so fleeting.

Over the next few days she grew to know him better as a doctor. She'd already seen him as a father, and as a friend. Now she saw him as a highly skilled professional, and she was impressed.

It wasn't only his medical skill that was so impressive, either. He was wonderful with the children, even during the sometimes painful procedures that were an inevitable part of a thorough examination. That didn't surprise her, because she'd seen him with Angel, but this was different.

He still cared passionately about their well-being, but he was detached enough to make rational decisions. Detached enough, when the time came, to know when to stop. That was something she'd always found hard, and this particular occasion was no different.

They had a child who had been knocked down by a car. She was horribly injured, her chest crushed, her spine damaged at several levels, and multiple fractures to all limbs. The paramedics had managed to get an IV line in in the helicopter, and she was splinted to a backboard from head to foot. Her extremities looked horrendous, but they were the least of her worries.

How she'd lived long enough to make it to the unit, Maddie didn't know. All she knew was that the child needed massive support to her circulatory and respiratory systems, and her pupils were unequal and fixed, and she was tiny and precious and almost certainly going to die.

Her parents were deranged with fear for her, and Maddie knew they had a right to be. Maureen brought them to Resus when they refused to stay away, and they stood by the doors, holding hands so hard their knuckles were white, their eyes fixed unblinking on Rob's every effort.

'We need to get her circulation boosted,' he muttered as they worked. 'She's hopelessly shocked. Her blood pressure doesn't even register half the time. She needs surgery fast. Is the surgical reg on his way?'

'Yes—coming now. He says any sign of abdominal trauma?'

Rob rolled his eyes slightly, so that only Maddie could see. The child had trauma everywhere. Her abdomen couldn't possibly have escaped injury. Maddie squeezed the bag of plasma expander and wondered how long the whole blood would take to come. They'd just used their stock of universal donor on a previous patient and their stocks hadn't been replenished yet.

'We need to get more into her, and fast. We need another line, and her arms are no go.'

'Circulation's too compromised in her legs,' Maddie told him quietly. 'There's no pulse on either side.'

He swore, very, very softly. 'We'll have to go into her neck on the other side. I didn't want to do that because of the collar.'

Spiro, the anaesthetist, came in and took over the top end, trying to establish a better airway and assess her consciousness, and the surgical reg arrived and went white.

Yes, Maddie thought, usually by the time you get them they've been sorted out a little, or we've lost them before you're called. Now you have to see it as it is.

And she wondered, with a lump in her throat, how the little girl's parents were faring in the corner with Maureen.

Rob was struggling to insert an IV into the collapsed neck veins of the child when the heart trace on the monitor hiccuped and went flat, triggering the alarm.

Maddie immediately locked her hands together over the child's breastbone, and then to her surprise Rob's hands covered hers, holding them still.

'What are you doing?' she asked blankly.

'Let her go,' he murmured.

'Do something!' the mother wept from behind them. 'Please, somebody, do something!'

She began to cry, huge, heart-rending sobs dragged up from the bottom of her soul, and Maddie stared into Rob's eyes and pleaded with him silently.

He shook his head, and Spiro put a hand on her shoulder and squeezed lightly. 'He's right, Maddie.'

How can he be right? she wanted to rage. She's the same age as Angel!

He turned towards the monitor and quietly switched it off. The silence was deafening, broken only by the harsh sobs of the little girl's mother and the tick of the clock on the wall. They'd been working on her for nearly an hour, she realised in shock. It had seemed like five minutes.

He turned towards the parents. 'I'm sorry,' he said heavily. 'Her injuries were too severe, too extensive—just too many to deal with.'

'You could have saved her!' the mother screamed, and Maureen hugged her and held her up. Her husband stood motionless, his eyes fixed on the child, all colour drained from his face.

'May I touch her?' he asked with devastating calm.

Rob nodded, and the man moved closer and stared down at her for an age, then bent and kissed her battered forehead. 'Tell me,' he said, his voice surprisingly strong. 'If she had survived, what would her life have been like?'

Rob looked at Spiro for confirmation. 'She was deeply unconscious. That might never have changed. Her left leg, certainly, and possibly her right arm would have been amputated because of damaged circulation and nerves, and she might have needed ventilation permanently because of her neck injuries. We don't know yet. Only a scan could show the exact degree of injury at each level, but it's likely she would have been quadriplegic and totally helpless.'

The man nodded. 'Thank you. That's what I thought.'

Then without looking again at the battered body of his daughter, he went out of the door, across the unit and out into the cold night.

Maureen took the mother to her office to let it sink in, and Maddie looked up at Rob with tears in her eyes. 'How could you?' she said. 'Did he need to know all that?'

'Yes.'

'You could have saved her.'

'No.'

'You could!'

Rob looked down at the little battered child between them and carefully, reverently, removed the IV line he'd been inserting. 'No,' he said softly. 'Maddie, on top of everything else she's got a pneumothorax and probably a ruptured heart. There's no skin on her back, she was dragged by the car. If she'd lived she would have faced years of agonising plastic and orthopaedic surgery, suffered almost total disability, her personality probably changed beyond recognition. There was no way we could save her, even if we'd wanted to. What she was, who she was, had already been destroyed. Sometimes life isn't the most important thing. You have to remember that.'

His words haunted her for the rest of the day.

It was ages later, at the end of her shift at nine o'clock, when Maddie saw Rob again to speak to. She'd just come off duty and he was waiting for her.

'Are you busy?'

She shook her head, still upset but needing to talk to him because she felt guilty for challenging his professional judgement, even though in her heart of hearts she knew he was right. 'I'm glad you're here. I wanted to apologise,' she said unevenly.

'There's no need. It was a tough call. It's just hard to let go of someone so tiny and precious.'

She looked up at him. 'I don't think we could have saved her anyway,' she said, and he gave a tiny, sad smile of agreement.

'Nor do I, but I didn't want to risk trying. It must be much easier to be a vet. You can be kind without everyone hating you or suing you.'

'I don't hate you!' Maddie said quickly, appalled that he should think it.

'Don't you? You did earlier.'

She shrugged helplessly. 'I just wasn't ready to let go. I'm sorry I questioned your judgement.'

His arm slipped round her shoulders and he hugged her gently. 'I've put Angel to bed. How about a quick drink and a bite to eat in the Newt?'

She flashed him a tired smile. 'I'm exhausted,' she confessed. 'I might just be able to stagger home if I go now.'

'Then let's go to the hospital canteen and have something, and I'll drive you home.'

She was almost tempted, but as much by the lift as anything, and it was beyond her to take advantage to that extent. 'I won't, thanks,' she told him.

'Sure?'

'Yes.'

His arm fell away, and she felt instantly cold and more alone. 'I'll see you in the morning, then,' he said.

She nodded, suppressing the urge to change her mind, and, flashing him a quick smile, she turned and strode briskly out of the unit, not letting herself slow down until she reached the front path of her house.

Then she let herself in, put the kettle on and opened her fridge. Nothing. She should have taken him up on his offer.

No. She shut the fridge, stuck a piece of bread in the toaster and sat down to wait. No food was very slimming. She'd comfort herself with that when she woke hungry in the night.

Better still, she'd have another bit of toast, she thought, and added jam to her shopping list under the frog magnet. The piece of paper that said 'New bra' fluttered to the floor and she scooped it up and shoved it in the bin. She'd find one tomorrow while she was out with Sarian.

'Oh, wow, what a wonderful shop!'

Sarian turned slowly round, staring open-mouthed at the amazing array of wedding dresses on offer. 'Oh, Maddie, we're in the wrong place. I really only want a very simple little dress—'

'That's fine. They have everything.' She turned and

caught the eye of a discreet sales assistant, who immediately came forward smiling a welcome.

'Can I help you, ladies?' she asked.

'Oh, we're just looking, thank you,' Sarian said a little weakly.

'Yes,' Maddie said firmly. 'My friend is getting married. She doesn't want anything fussy, no frills or meringue—just something quietly elegant.'

The assistant looked searchingly at Sarian. 'Long or short, my dear?'

'Oh—on the knee, probably. Just a day dress.'

'Cream, with your lovely colouring?'

'Yes, I think so. White's a bit—'

'Bridal?' Maddie said drily.

Sarian gave a wry smile. 'I just don't want to look—overdone.'

The assistant nodded understandingly. 'How about winter white? There are some lovely dresses in our new stock. So many brides these days just want to look chic. There are so many second weddings, too. It's made for much more choice. How about this?'

She pulled a dress from a rail, and Sarian shook her head. 'I don't like that neckline. Something more—' She gestured at her throat, drawing a line with her fingertips above the swell of her breasts.

The assistant delved again, coming out with a slash neckline. No. A cowl? No.

'How about this?' Maddie asked, lifting one off another rail and holding it up. It was very simple, just a straight little shift of the finest wool crêpe, sleeveless, with a discreet little sweetheart neckline and a scatter of tiny pearls over one shoulder and across the bodice.

'It's lovely,' Sarian said longingly.

'Try it.'

She shook her head. 'It won't suit me. I'm too fat—'

'There isn't an ounce on you!' Maddie said crossly. 'You're gorgeous. Try it.'

'But it drapes!'

'Mmm. Lovely. Elegant. Put it on.'

Doubtfully, Sarian disappeared into the fitting room, emerging a moment later looking pleased and surprised.

'It fits,' she said, her voice slightly stunned.

'Annie, you look fantastic,' Maddie said sincerely, a lump forming in her throat. 'It's lovely.'

Sarian twirled, looking at her back in the mirror over her shoulder. 'Do you think so?'

'It's perfect—stand here and look. There are mirrors all around you,' the assistant told her, and she and Maddie stood back and admired the simple, elegant little dress.

'With your hair up, perhaps, and maybe the jacket? The dress has a lovely little lacy cardigan with pearls set in it to match the motif on the front—'

She handed her a little slither of silky cream lace scattered with pearls, and Sarian slipped her arms into it and stood back.

'Perfect. Now, accessories. A hat?'

'No. I don't think so. I'm not a hat person. Perhaps a flower?'

'Good idea. Now, how about shoes?'

'I've got some gold ones—little pumps. Would they do?'

'Annie, it's your wedding!' Maddie scolded. 'You can always wear the shoes again.'

So she tried on shoes, little simple courts that finished the outfit. There were tights, too, glossy ones that were just perfect, and she put them on one side with the shoes.

Sarian did a final twirl, then went and changed, coming out of the fitting room with her eyes sparkling. 'I feel it's really going to happen now,' she said, the excitement in her voice telling Maddie more clearly than anything else how much her forthcoming wedding meant to her.

'I'm so happy for you,' Maddie said softly, and hugged her. 'You're going to look beautiful, and he's going to be so proud of you.'

Her friend's eyes misted, and she hugged Maddie back. 'Thanks,' she whispered in a choked voice. Then she straightened and sniffed and managed a wobbly smile. 'You'll set me off in a minute,' she chided, and went to pay for her dress.

While she was busy with the assistant, Maddie scanned the rows of beautiful dresses, and her eye was caught by a lovely oyster silk with a heavily embroidered bodice, the front of the waist tapering to a plunging vee, and a wonderful skirt that fanned out into a mock train behind. There was more embroidery down the back of the train, and on the cuffs of the slender sleeves, and Maddie knew without a shadow of a doubt that it was the dress for her.

'That's gorgeous,' Sarian said. 'Why don't you try it on?'

Part of her wanted to, but she couldn't bring herself to lie to the assistant, or to indulge herself so fruitlessly. She shook her head. 'No. It's getting late.'

'Get a ball gown—they've got some here, on the other side. You ought to have a new dress, you've only got that one in your wardrobe and I know for a fact you've had it for years.'

Maddie laughed dismissively, still aching about the wedding dress. 'There's no point. There's years of life left in my green one. I don't need another.'

'But you're going with Rob!'

'Only because Daniel volunteered him to get us out of a fix,' Maddie reminded her. 'And anyway, I can't afford it this month. I had to have my car serviced.'

'I don't know why you bother to have that car, keeping it at your parents' house. It seems so silly having it miles away.'

'Only two miles, and it's so I can escape when I want to,' Maddie told her. 'Right, are you ready?'

Sarian nodded. 'I asked about Angel, too. We have to measure her and ring up, and they'll put things out that are her size and she can try them on at Rob's. They hire or sell them.'

'She might want to keep it,' Maddie said. 'We'd better let Rob decide.'

They hailed a taxi and went back to the flat, hanging up the lovely dress in Sarian's wardrobe.

'Put on that ball gown,' Sarian said firmly, but Maddie refused. She knew her friend would tell her that it was out of date and not a wonderful fit, but she didn't intend to do anything about it.

Rob was only taking her because Daniel had left him no choice, and he was too much of a gentleman to refuse. No doubt they'd have a pleasant enough evening, but there was no need to go mad.

'Are you coming to the ball?' Maddie asked Sarian to distract her. 'It's your wedding night.'

'We'll pop in, but I doubt if we'll stay long. Do you think the dress would be all right?'

'Lovely,' Maddie assured her. 'Quite suitable, and very pretty. You could let your hair down, maybe, or change the shoes.'

'I still think that green dress is too old—'

'Tough,' Maddie said firmly. 'It's what I'm wearing. Right, I'm having a cup of tea and going to bed.'

And hopefully, she thought, I won't spend the night dreaming about that beautiful wedding dress and how I'll never need it…

Angel was ecstatic when Rob told her she was to be a bridesmaid at Daniel's wedding. Even through the bandages he could see the delight on her face, and when Maddie and Sarian brought the little dresses for her to try, she was so excited he thought she would burst.

Daniel swung her gently up into the air and kissed her nose, then hugged her and turned to Sarian. 'Darling, I want you to meet a very special little girl. Angel, this is Sarian, and we're getting married next weekend.'

'And I'm going to be your bridesmaid!' Angel trilled.

Sarian smiled. 'That's right. Thank you so much for agreeing. I don't have a little sister or cousin to ask, and nor does Daniel, so we were a bit disappointed because we couldn't have a bridesmaid, but now we have! Are you looking forward to it?'

Angel nodded, squiggling in Daniel's arms and trying to see the dresses. 'Are they for me to try?' she asked, peering round his shoulder at the heap of plastic garment bags Maddie had brought in.

'Yes,' Sarian told her, and Daniel put her down so she could go and look at them.

One by one they were unzipped and pulled out, and she was so excited she could hardly stand still while they put them on her.

She loved them all, but one in particular seemed to fit her to perfection. It was a glorious deep red velvet, stunning with her dark eyes and hair, and had a pretty little sweetheart neckline that echoed the dress Sarian had chosen.

She looked wonderful in it, and Rob felt his heart melt. She would be pale and pasty after all that time with the bandages, and it would lend her a bit of colour. She could wear it for Christmas, as well, as it was ballerina length. Not that they'd be doing anything very much at Christmas, but perhaps there would be parties she could go to.

'Do you like that dress?' Rob asked her.

'I love it!' she whispered, staring wide-eyed at her reflection. 'May I have it, Daddy, please? I'll be so pretty in it.'

It sounded almost like a promise, and his heart wrenched again. She was so obsessed with prettiness. Didn't she understand how much he loved her?

'I'm sure you will, and of course you can have it, if Sarian likes it.'

'Sarian loves it,' Sarian said. 'In fact, I think I might be just a tiny bit jealous.'

Her smiled softened the words, and when she held out her arms Angel flew into them and hugged her. Always affectionate and open, she'd been positively reclusive since the accident, and this was the first time she'd shown any real sign of her old self.

He looked at Daniel, and saw a strange expression in his eyes, a mixture of longing and adoration that chilled him.

Did he know? Was that it? Was Angel his, and he'd known all this time?

Rob looked away, swallowing bile. He'd told himself it didn't matter. He'd almost managed to convince himself, as well.

But it did matter—not that she was his, but that she wasn't Daniel's. He'd already resigned himself to the fact that Maria might have deliberately sought him out as a stooge because she was already pregnant with another man's child.

That didn't matter to Rob. He loved Angel for herself, and her true parentage was, to a certain extent, irrelevant.

But if Angel was Daniel's, it was different. She saw him all the time, regarded him as an honorary uncle. They had a relationship—and it might be the wrong one.

If Angel was Daniel's, then Rob had to know. He didn't know how it would change things, or even if it would, but the uncertainty was beginning to eat at him, and he was damned if he would be kept in ignorance if Daniel knew already.

All he had to do was ask him, and that was the hardest thing of all.

CHAPTER SEVEN

THE cake smelt gorgeous. Maddie sniffed it appreciatively, drizzled another good measure of brandy onto the base to hasten the maturing process, and wrapped it up again.

She was hassling it a bit, but she had no choice. It was already Monday, and she had six days left to cover it in marzipan, let it set and then ice it with a smooth layer of icing, then decorate the icing once it had hardened.

She didn't mind, she loved icing cakes and she was good at it, but she wished she had more time to do it justice. She'd been on duty over the weekend, and when she'd arrived home her mother had rung up to ask her when she was going over.

'Soon,' she'd promised, and because she loved them and missed them and their nagging, she'd agreed to go the following Sunday, the day after the wedding and the Friends' ball.

Then she'd fallen into bed, and remembered she'd missed putting brandy on the cake.

That was why she was here, in Rob's flat, at six-thirty on Monday morning, with her nerves at attention because he was wandering around in a short towelling robe flashing the sexiest legs she'd seen in years and messing up her blood pressure and her mind.

He came out of the bathroom just as she put the lid back on the tin, and sniffed the air.

'Bit early, isn't it?' he said with a grin, and she grinned back.

'Bad weekend,' she told him, brandishing the bottle. 'I thought it would kick-start the week.'

He chuckled and wandered back into the bathroom, then stuck his head out again. 'I don't suppose you want to put the kettle on? I could murder a coffee.'

'At six-thirty?' she squeaked in disgust. 'Yuck! How can you do that to yourself?'

He lounged on the doorframe, a smile playing around his lips. 'Don't tell me—you're a tea person.'

'You know that already,' she said, trying not to notice the runnels of water streaming off his wet hair and dribbling down his neck into the hollow of his throat. His legs were damp, too, the hair glistening with beads of water from the shower that had tormented her with unbidden images while she did the cake.

She pushed the tin back into the cupboard and picked up the kettle. 'I'll make you coffee,' she said with an exaggerated sigh, hoping he hadn't noticed her protracted inspection of his body.

'You're a love,' he murmured, and went into the bathroom, shutting the door.

She shook her head to clear it, and filled the kettle, made a mug of instant coffee with whitener from the jars in the corner and slipped out before he emerged.

A woman could only stand so much!

Angel's stitches were due out on Wednesday, and Rob had arranged with Daniel for cover so that he could be there. He was dreading it. What if Angel wasn't satisfied with the result? She was so worried about her face, and he couldn't cope with her disappointment if the surgery hadn't managed a miracle.

He was up at the ward at six, helping her bath and dress, sharing her breakfast to encourage her to eat even though he didn't have any appetite either.

Peggie appeared at eight, and Gareth a few moments later. 'All set?' he said, and Angel nodded soberly. She was as taut as a steel hawser, and Rob thought he was going to be sick with the tension.

They unravelled the bandages, a little grubby now after nearly two weeks, and lifted away the thick padding of wool and paraffin gauze.

'Right, Angel, I'd like you to sit here,' Gareth said, indicating a chair on one side of a little table, then indicated one on the other side and added, 'and I'm going to sit here, and we're going to lean on our elbows and sit as still as possible and I'm going to take out all of these tiny little stitches one by one, and it's going to be very boring and take ages and you're going to have to help me to count. All right? And according to Dad, you can have a chocolate button for every one. He can put them out in little rows for you and you'll have to make sure he doesn't cheat and eat any.'

Angel gave a tiny giggle, and Gareth winked conspiratorially and turned to Rob. 'Pull up a chair and sit beside her. Then she can hold your hand and squeeze it once for every stitch. And watch him,' he told Angel deadpan. 'You'll have to make sure he can count.'

Rob sat beside her, squeezing her hand on the table. Gareth was full of tricks, and finding a way to have them holding hands was very welcome, because Rob was worried. Worried sick that once the tiny black spiders all over her face had been removed, the scars would be no better than before. At the moment it was hard to tell, and he didn't dare let his optimism get the better of him too soon.

He opened the chocolate buttons to give himself something to do, grateful that Maddie had suggested this little trick. The surgeon finished washing his hands and putting on gloves, and then settled down in the chair opposite Angel and picked up a scalpel. 'Right, Angel, I'm going to take these stitches out now and I need you to be very still. All right? Ready to count?'

She nodded almost imperceptibly, and Gareth rested his elbows on the table and leant forwards. 'Can you see my eyebrows?' he asked.

'Yes.'

'Right. I'll snip, and you count, and if I hurt you, you can pull one of the hairs out of my eyebrows as a punishment.'

She giggled, and he winked again and then settled down. 'OK. Hold still, now.'

It took ages, and Rob was waiting for her to cry out or wince or flinch, but she didn't move a muscle except to nudge him if he was a bit slow putting out a chocolate button. Once or twice Gareth straightened and stretched, giving her a chance to fidget, and then he continued.

Rob couldn't see what he was doing, because the consultant was working on the other side of her face, but the suspense was killing him.

Then finally, when he thought he was going to scream, Gareth sat back, smiled slightly and handed the scalpel to a nurse. 'There. All out, and I didn't lose any eyebrows. What a lot of chocolate drops!'

She looked down at the rows of brown buttons and her eyes widened. 'Wow!' she said.

'I expect you'll be sick,' Rob said drily.

'Did I really have so many stitches?'

'Unless your dad can't count. Smile for me?'

Angel's mouth tipped in a tentative and humourless plastic smile, and Gareth's mouth tipped down at the corners in response.

'Is that the best smile you can find for me this morning, even with all those chocolate buttons?' he said mournfully, and she giggled and her whole face smiled in response.

'Better. That's lovely. Open your mouth a little? Good. Excellent. Right, we need to wash that grubby little face that hasn't seen a flannel for two weeks, and then we can put some little paper stitches on like tiny plasters, just to help the skin stay in the right place. OK?'

She nodded, and Gareth moved out of the way so the nurse could clean her skin. While she waited for the nurse to prepare everything, Angel ate a couple of chocolate buttons and turned very hesitantly to Rob.

'Is it all right?' she asked anxiously, her voice scarcely more than a whisper.

Rob studied her face, one side of it covered with a tracery of fine red lines where the incisions had been made, and sighed with relief. 'It's excellent. It's really good. You'll be pleased.' I hope, he added silently. She was so critical of herself these days.

'Right, let's sort you out,' the nurse said, settling down with a tray of equipment in front of her.

'What's all that?' Angel asked.

'Just the things I need. First I'm going to bathe

your face with distilled water, then put on a nice gentle cream to moisturise it where it's dried up, and then we'll put on some little Steri-Strip plasters. Then every day you'll have it creamed to keep it lovely and soft, and at night you'll wear a little sleep mask to keep it all nice and still while you wiggle about in your sleep. OK?'

'I don't wiggle,' Angel said with a superior look.

'Is that right? Well, how amazing. I thought everybody wiggled.'

'Worms wiggle,' Angel told her, eating another button. 'And snakes.'

Rob sat back and surreptitiously eased the kinks out of his shoulders. The tension was killing him, because she had yet to see her face, and he just knew she would be disappointed.

He was right. Even though she gave a dutiful little smile and peered this way and that in the mirror, Rob could tell she wasn't satisfied. Of course she still had the fine red lines of the incisions, and until they faded she would still be very conscious of them, and the little pink paper sutures that held the skin to give extra support were also slightly noticeable.

Nevertheless, it was a huge improvement on the puckered scars she'd had before, and he was delighted for her.

'The lines will fade, Angel,' he said encouragingly. 'It's nice to see you again. I've missed you under all those bandages!'

She looked unsmilingly at him out of sombre eyes. 'I don't have a pretty smile any more,' she said. 'Only one side. The other side's got all lines on it.'

'But it's straight now,' he pointed out. 'It's much better, and once it's all healed properly both sides will be pretty. And both sides move together now. It won't show soon, you'll see. It'll be wonderful.'

'Not for the wedding,' she told him sadly.

He hugged her gently, cradling her face against his shirt with infinite care, and dropped a loving kiss on the top of her little head. Poor baby. 'You'll be beautiful for the wedding,' he told her firmly. 'Sarian and Daniel will be proud of you, and you'll be lovely in that new dress.'

'I can keep it, can't I?' she said, twisting round to look up at him. 'For later, when I'm pretty?'

'Darling, you're pretty now,' he told her, his voice choked. 'More than pretty enough for me. I'm just glad you're alive.'

She studied him for a moment, then wrapped her arms around him and hugged him hard with her skinny little arms. 'So will you still be my daddy?'

'Of course I will. I told you that.'

And I wish I believed it, he thought despairingly.

He had to speak to Daniel.

'So that's what you look like! Well, it's really nice to meet you at last,' Maddie said with a smile, and, plopping down on the chair beside her bed, she handed Angel a little box of chocolates.

'Are these for me?' Angel said, awed.

'Yup. A little bird told me you were a brave girl this morning.' Maddie settled herself more comfortably on the chair and prodded the box with her finger. 'You're allowed to open them. It's customary to share chocolates with the person that gives them to you.'

Angel giggled and opened the box, peeling the Cellophane away with enormous care and deliberation. While she was busy Maddie studied Gareth's handiwork and marvelled. Either Rob had exaggerated her degree of scarring, or the man was a miracle worker.

Yes, the marks were still visible, but there was no puckering or pulling, and the skin seemed to move equally on both sides of her face. Only when she smiled did it show in a slight stiffness on one side of her mouth, but Maddie imagined that might disappear with time.

Finally Angel broke into the box of chocolates, and handed them to Maddie. 'You choose first,' she said, and Maddie picked out the marzipan, because children universally hated marzipan and coffee creams. That was her next choice.

She leant forwards, her head near Angel's, and whispered, 'I've got a job for you.'

Angel looked at her through her fringe. 'What?' she stage-whispered back.

Maddie looked round, then leant closer. 'Will you help me decorate the wedding cake?'

The child's eyes widened. 'Me?' she squeaked.

Maddie nodded. 'Please? I need someone to help spread the jam, and stick the marzipan on the outside, and then I'll need someone to help me put flowers on little blobs of icing all over the top—little rice-paper flowers. It's a secret,' she added, and Angel nodded, eyes still like saucers.

'When?' she asked.

'What's all the whispering about?' Rob said, hunching down beside them and joining in.

'Maddie wants me to help ice the wedding cake,' she hissed excitedly. 'For Daniel and Sa-Sara—' She looked at Maddie for help.

'Sarian,' she supplied. 'I need another pair of hands.'

Rob met her eyes, his own filled with gratitude. 'I'm sure she'd love that,' he said warmly.

'Tonight?'

'I'm on call,' he said regretfully.

'But I'm not. You don't have to be there. We can manage if you have to go, can't we, darling?'

Angel nodded, and Maddie wondered if she'd imagined it or if there really was disappointment in Rob's eyes. If there was, he masked it quickly. 'Fine,' he said. 'Get the key off me if I'm busy, and take Angel over there. You know the code?'

Maddie nodded and stood up. 'I'll see you about six—and remember, not a word!'

Angel pressed her finger to her lips, and Maddie winked at her, ruffled her hair and pinched the coffee cream. 'You can have the rest,' she said with a grin, and left them to it.

She had all the ingredients she needed in a bag in her locker, and she was looking forward to starting the decorating. Rob had booked the hotel room, just a short distance away overlooking Regent's Park, and although she'd agreed to share the cost she had the distinct feeling he was blotting up most of the bill.

Ah, well, she might not have much money, but she could give them a cake to remember.

She went back to the A and E department, grabbed a cup of coffee and a biscuit and went out to the central work station. 'What's going on, then?' she asked everyone. 'Busy?'

'Dead as a dodo,' Charity said. 'They're saving it all up for when you go off duty.'

Maddie laughed and settled onto a stool, cradling her coffee. 'I approve.'

'How's Angel?' Daniel asked, sidling up to her and stealing the rest of her biscuit.

'Wonderful. She looks super. Rob's pleased. Of course, I don't know what he was dealing with, but Gareth seems to have done a wonderful job.'

'They're getting married on Saturday morning,' someone said. 'Isn't that nice? Peggie's such a love.'

'She'd need to be—he's a bit crusty.'

'I think he's really kind. He's wonderful with the children,' Maddie said thoughtfully. 'It's funny how many people we have like that.'

'Like Maureen, you mean?' Jenny Barber said drily.

'She's an excellent nurse,' Daniel defended.

'While we're on the gossip, do you remember Amanda Grayson from Outpatients who married Edward Burrows in March?' Charity said.

'She started her maternity leave last month, didn't she?' Jenny put in. 'They moved to a new house in Epping Forest.'

'That's right. Well, they've just had twin boys!'

'Oh, that's wonderful!' Jenny said, obviously delighted.

'You think so? I'd hate twins.' Charity grimaced. 'All that double trouble! Although sometimes I think the chance would be nice!'

'There's a new guy in Orthopaedics—have you seen him?' Jenny asked her.

'Black?'

'Not that it matters, but yes.'

Charity sat up straighter. 'Single?'

She nodded.

'Big?'

'Pray for a fracture to come in, you might find out.'

Charity smiled. 'I might do that. God owes me one at the moment.'

The red phone jangled, and they all glared at Charity.

'If that's your doing,' Daniel said threateningly, and Maddie scooped up the phone.

'A and E.'

'School party coming in—nausea, vomiting, stomach cramps—they've all gone down like flies in the last half-hour. Expect about fifteen or so, please.'

Maddie cradled the receiver and looked at Charity. 'You're safe. It's school kids with vomiting.'

Charity laughed. 'There's safe and there's safe. I would have plunked for the fracture!'

They were working flat out for the next two hours, sorting out the school group who had clearly eaten something nasty in their Christmas party menu. It was too quick for salmonella, but was clearly some form of contamination.

They washed faces and hands, held bowls, set up IV lines, changed sheets and monitored the little scraps while they cried and retched and cuddled their tummies, and before long most of the parents had arrived and were able to take over the cleaning-up operation to free the hospital staff so they could do their real job—treating the children.

Finally they were under control. Several were better, some were showing slight signs of recovery, and only two had been admitted for further treatment and observation.

Then the nurse on triage popped her head round the corner and caught Maddie's eye.

'I've got a toddler with a fracture—he fell down the stairs and caught his arm in the banisters. Can someone see him?'

Charity's head flew up. 'The fracture's mine,' she said firmly, and everyone chuckled.

She appeared moments later with a tall, dark man in his late twenties, big and burly, a whimpering child cradled tenderly against his chest, and Charity ushered them into a cubicle.

Rob signed the X-ray form after his initial examination showed an obvious displacement in the forearm, and Charity escorted them to the X-ray room, and then contacted the orthopaedic registrar Jenny had been talking about.

They all carried on with their work, watching Charity out of the corners of their eyes, and after the new Orthopaedics man had come down, examined the baby and decided to admit him for surgery for reduction of the fracture, Charity escorted them up to theatre.

'You're right, he's gorgeous,' someone said to Jenny in an undertone, just to Maddie's right. Maddie, though, didn't think Charity had even noticed him.

The school group were finished and sorted out and the team were in the staff room grabbing a well-earned cup of tea by the time she reappeared.

Jenny looked up and said, 'Well?' impatiently.

'What?' Charity said, looking wary.

'What did you think of the new guy?'

Maddie would have sworn she blushed under that flawless ebony skin. 'I didn't really notice him.'

'Liar!' they all cried.

'I didn't. I was too busy.'

Maddie studied her closely. 'With the father,' she put in quietly.

This time she definitely blushed. 'He's a single parent—his wife's left him. He's really sweet. He's a university lecturer. His name's David.' She finally ran out of steam and looked around helplessly.

'And?' Jenny prompted.

'I'm going round for dinner tomorrow night.'

There was a chorus of cheers, and Maddie drained her coffee and stood up with a smile. 'Excellent. I hope you have a lovely time. Right, I have to go and entertain Angel so she doesn't scratch her face. I'll see you all tomorrow.'

She left them, wondering as she walked briskly home in the darkening streets if this man could be the one Charity had been waiting for. She was a darling, and Maddie wished she could find someone to love.

Someone like Rob, she thought, and nearly tripped over the kerb.

Rob?

Someone to love?

She paused for a moment in the lea of a hedge, and wondered what on earth she was getting herself into. He'd given her no indication that he felt anything for her other than friendship and a very casual interest. She must be mad to imagine she loved him.

Good grief, she didn't know him well enough!

Somehow she didn't think that was going to stop her foolish heart from doing its own thing.

'That's lovely. Right, we can leave it to dry till tomorrow, and then we can put the white on the outside, then on Friday we can put the flowers on and make it all ready for Saturday. Are you looking forward to it?'

Angel nodded at Maddie, her eyes sparkling. 'I'm going to wear my pretty dress.' Her face clouded a little, and Maddie, now attuned to her expressions, prompted her gently.

'Are we going to put flowers in your hair like before?'

'I s'pose,' she said quietly. 'Will I look pretty enough then?'

Maddie sighed softly. 'Darling, you're very pretty anyway. Pretty enough for what?'

'For Daddy to still love me. Mummy said—'

She trailed off, and Maddie waited.

'Yes?'

'She said he only loved me because I was pretty. She said if I wasn't so pretty, he wouldn't love me. She said he probably wasn't my real daddy anyway, but I don't understand. Why isn't he? Is it because I'm not pretty now?'

And to Maddie's horror, she started to cry, scrubbing at her eyes and rubbing perilously close to the suture line. Poor little scrap doesn't understand, she thought, she's far too young to comprehend the concept of real and natural fathers.

'Darling, don't rub your face. Come here,' she ordered gently, and drew the child onto her lap, cuddling her and rocking her until the storm of weeping subsided.

'Now,' she said quietly, tucking Angel into the crook of her arm and snuggling her against the soft cushion of her breasts. 'I don't understand why your mother might have said anything like that to you, but all I know is that your father loves you. Really, truly loves you. He worries about you all the time, and he couldn't love you more if you were made of solid gold. All that matters to him is that you're well, and you're getting better.'

Angel tipped up her face and looked at Maddie through tear-drenched eyes. 'Really?'

'Really. Now, it's getting late. Do you want me to take you over to the ward and help put you to bed?'

Angel nodded. 'Daddy's busy. He's always busy, but he has to help the other children, too.'

'That's right. Most fathers have to go to work. At least he's near.'

'Mmm. Can I have another of my chocolates before I go to bed?'

'Only if you clean your teeth afterwards and promise not to be sick. I didn't realise you'd have so many chocolate buttons this morning or I wouldn't have given them to you. I'd have found something else.'

Angel smiled impishly. 'I'm glad you didn't. Let's go and have some more.'

And Maddie, who badly needed a chocolate fix, readily agreed.

They weren't there. He leant against the door, too tired to move, and after a few minutes he heard Maddie's footsteps on the stairs.

'I went to A and E to give you these, but you'd left,' she told him, handing him the keys.

He dredged up a smile. 'Thanks. How's Angel?'

'Still worrying,' Maddie murmured, reluctant to cause him concern.

'Not the "if I'm pretty you'll be my daddy" thing again?'

She nodded.

'Oh, hell,' he said tiredly, and opened the door of the flat. 'Coffee?'

'No, I'm tired. I've got to sort out my washing. Thanks, though.'

'Thank you. I'm sure Angel enjoyed doing the cake. Is it finished?'

Maddie laughed. 'No—it'll take two more days— or nights, rather. Luckily I'm on earlies for the rest of the week, so I can do it in the evening with Angel.'

He nodded, then, without any further reason to keep her there, he said goodnight and watched her leave.

Closing the door softly, he sat down and stared blankly into space. He had to talk to Daniel. He had to sort this thing out once and for all, but not tonight. Not when they might be interrupted. He reached for his mobile phone and rang Daniel.

'Are you busy tomorrow evening?' he said shortly.

'No,' Daniel said after a tiny pause. 'Why?'

'I thought we could have a drink.'

'A stag night?' his friend said incredulously.

Damn. He'd almost forgotten about the wedding. 'Not exactly. Here? Seven?'

'Sounds fine. Want to give me any clues?'

'Not really.'

He said goodbye and cut the connection, then went into the bathroom, stripped off his clothes and turned on the shower. At least the water was always hot, he thought, standing numbly under the powerful spray and letting the water wash away the stains and troubles of the day.

And this time tomorrow, he'd have an answer.

'What's this all about?' Daniel asked bluntly.

The door had hardly closed behind him before he'd

asked the question, and Rob, who had been casting around for days to find a way to raise the subject, gave up his carefully rehearsed speeches and met the eyes of the man who had been his friend for years. The man who was Angel's friend—and maybe more.

'Are you Angel's father?' he said abruptly.

Daniel's eyes widened in shock. 'What? Of course I'm not. What on earth made you think that?'

Rob scrubbed his hands through his hair and turned away, staring blindly at the ceiling. 'Maria said something to Angel. She said I might not be her father. She said, "It was Easy."' He turned. 'I have to know the truth, Daniel. Please. Don't lie to me, no matter what it is. I have to know.'

For an age, Daniel was silent, searching Rob's face, then he seemed to come to a decision. 'I'm going to tell you something. I don't want to do this, and I'll only say it if you promise me it's the last time you'll bring it up.'

Rob nodded. 'I promise.'

He hesitated, then drew a steadying breath. 'There's no way Angel can be my child. There's only one person in the world who could ever be the mother of my child, because I have never made love to anyone else. Not Maria, not anyone—until I met Sarian.'

Rob stared at him, shocked. True, he'd always come home at night, but Rob had thought it was simply a preference for sleeping alone. It had never occurred to him that his friend had held himself aloof from all physical relationships, and the knowledge stunned him.

'My God,' he said softly. 'No one?'

Daniel shook his head. 'So, you see, whoever her father is, it isn't me.'

Rob felt his shoulders drop a mile, and sudden emotion clogged his throat. He looked up at Daniel and dredged for a smile. 'I'm sorry. I just felt—if you were, or could be her father—you ought to know. Angel ought to know.'

'And you ought to know,' he said gently, then went on, 'What if it's someone else?'

'I don't care.'

'Liar.'

The words were soft, but they cut him to the quick. Tears sprang to his eyes, and he turned away. 'I love her. It doesn't matter. I'll always love her.'

'Of course you will, but I'm sure you're her father. She's so like you, Rob.'

'Like me?' he said with a strangled laugh. 'She's the spitting image of Maria.'

'No. She's got Maria's hair and eye colour, but she's got your mouth, your chin, your eyes.'

Rob looked at the mirror doubtfully. 'You think so?'

'It shows when you laugh.'

Rob gave a wry snort. 'I can't remember. I don't think I've laughed for years.'

'What's her blood group?' Daniel asked, changing tack.

'A positive.'

'And yours?'

'The same.'

'And Maria's?'

'O positive.'

'And I'm AB negative—I'm on the police register for emergency donations. I couldn't possibly be her father. Only another man with A positive blood group could be, you know that—and there aren't many of you about. Does that give you enough proof?'

Rob shook his head and gave a rueful smile. 'I didn't need any more. At least not from you—not now. No one would lie about a thing like that.'

He hesitated, then met Daniel's eyes apologetically. 'Easy, I'm sorry I doubted you, but Angel was so convinced I wouldn't be her father if she wasn't pretty, and whatever Maria said to her seems to have made her believe that I'm not, and that I'm only around because the kid's cute—'

He broke off, choked again with anger at Maria and pain for Angel, and a moment later Daniel stepped forwards and gave him a fierce, awkward hug.

'Forget it, Rob,' he said, sounding choked himself. 'I know you're her father. I can see it a mile away. Stop torturing yourself and get on with loving the kid. She's yours. Be proud of her.'

Rob nodded. 'I am. Thanks.' He picked up a wine bottle from the cupboard in the corner and waved it at Daniel. 'Drink?'

Daniel gave a slow, lazy smile. 'Just one—I'm supposed to be taking Sarian out to dinner later. I said I'll call her if I couldn't go.'

Rob handed him a glass of red wine, and lifted his own. 'Let's drink to her—she must be something special.'

Daniel's eyes softened. 'She is. She's the only person I've ever met who I've felt able to open up to.'

'What about Maddie? You've talked about her so much I would have thought you'd open up with her.'

He shook his head. 'No. It's different. We don't

ask questions or expect confessions—we just offer support and friendship. She's a lovely woman, but she's not the woman for me.'

'And Sarian is.'

'And Sarian is. Quite definitely.'

'Worth waiting for?'

Daniel gave a slight smile, his eyes revealing more than he could know. 'Oh, yes,' he said softly. 'Every minute of the last thirty-two years.'

'You're a lucky man,' Rob said gruffly, and raised his glass. 'To Sarian,' he murmured. 'I hope you'll be very happy together. You deserve it.'

CHAPTER EIGHT

SARIAN looked worried. Well, perhaps not worried, but certainly puzzled. She'd picked up her post on the way out that morning, and Maddie had just watched her scan a sheet of paper in a stolen moment, and stuff it into her pocket.

Maddie put the pile of X-ray requests into the rack in Cubicle Four and went over to her. 'Everything OK, Annie?' she asked, concerned.

'I've had a letter,' Sarian said, sounding bemused. 'From my parents' solicitors. They want to me to contact them as soon as possible—they've been trying to get hold of me for months, apparently, since shortly after they died. I didn't leave a forwarding address— well, there wasn't a lot of point when they'd written me out of their wills, was there?'

'So what's it about?' Maddie asked, as puzzled as Sarian.

She shrugged. 'Search me. I have no idea. It could be anything. They might have found something of mine in the house, I suppose, although I doubt it after all these years. I haven't been there for such a long time—not since I was seventeen, except for that last visit just before they died. Oh, Lord, Maddie, what is it all about?'

'Ring them,' Maddie said.

'It's not even eight o'clock. They won't be there.'

'So ring them at nine.'

She nodded, fingering the letter in her pocket as if

135

she could divine its meaning by contact. 'Oh, well, we might as well get on. Looks like they've had a busy night—everything needs restocking.'

'Yes, and I can hear the waiting room hotting up. I'll pop out and see what's just come in. I don't like the sound of that screaming child.'

She went through one of the cubicles and scanned the busy waiting area. The child in question was lying across his father's lap, screaming and drawing up his legs, and the man was rocking him and talking soothingly to him while an anxious woman, obviously the mother, talked urgently to the receptionist.

Maddie crossed over to them. 'Can I help you?' she asked.

The woman wheeled round and looked at Maddie. 'Are you a nurse?'

'Yes. I'm Sister Brooks. Is that your baby?'

She nodded. 'He's been crying for ages, off and on, and he's started being sick, and I thought he just had a tummy bug, but he's got worse—'

'Let's get him looked at, then,' she said, picking up the notes from the receptionist and ushering them through into a cubicle. 'Just sit down with him on your lap and I'll get a doctor to see him straight away.'

She went round the corner and found Rob, just coming out of another cubicle.

'I've got a little boy who's just come in,' she said softly. 'He looks like a classic intestinal obstruction—either that or enterocolitis. He looks pale and shocky, and he's got intermittent colicky pain and vomiting.'

'Is that him screaming?'

'Yes. I thought he needed urgent attention. Can you see him now?'

Rob nodded. 'OK. Let's have a look.' He went into the cubicle and introduced himself to the parents, then, crouching down in front of the father with a smile, he ran his eyes over the boy without touching, just assessing his appearance while he said hello.

The boy just looked at him listlessly, and turned away, burying his face in his father's shirt. Rob laid a hand gently on his head, assessing his temperature, and was just reaching for his wrist to check his pulse when the boy stiffened.

Another bout of screaming started, and just in the nick of time Maddie grabbed a paper bowl and popped it under his chin. 'Bile,' Rob murmured, then, raising his voice, he turned to the parents. 'Is he constipated?' he asked.

'Oh—well, I don't know. Yes, possibly,' the mother said. 'He's going on his own now, so I don't always know. Oh, dear. Is it his appendix?'

'I don't think so,' Rob said loudly over the screams. 'I'd like to have a look at him when this bout of pain subsides. Perhaps you could lie him on your lap?'

The boy started to relax after a moment, and quickly the father laid him down and Rob pulled his clothes out of the way and gently felt all over his tummy.

'Hmm. OK, I think I'd like to get someone else to have a look at him, if you don't mind? I don't think it's his appendix, but he may have an obstruction of some sort, and I think he could need surgery urgently to sort him out.'

The boy's mother looked panic-stricken. 'He will be all right, won't he? I mean—he won't—oh, God!'

'No. It's highly unlikely that it's anything life

threatening. I'd lay odds on a bit of gut getting twisted up or a swallowed object like a toy. I'll get someone down to look at him now, and then once they've decided if they're going to operate we'll give him some pain relief, because we don't want him suffering any longer than is necessary.'

He looked at Maddie. 'In the meantime I think we need bloods for Us and Es, haemoglobin, cross matching and I think we'll start him on a saline drip. He's a bit shocky, as you said.' He turned to the parents again.

'I know it's a shot in the dark, but you haven't been to the Tropics recently, have you?'

'Well—yes, we have,' the father said. 'I was working on an engineering project until six months ago, in Nigeria. Why?'

'Because he looks a little anaemic. It might be worms.'

'But we wormed him regularly!' the mother said indignantly.

'Just a thought. Wormers don't always work— sometimes if there are a lot of worms they just make a plug. We'll do an X-ray once we've taken the bloods, to see if that sheds any more light on it.'

The X-ray revealed a diffuse ball of tissue, and the general surgeon who came down recommended exploratory surgery without delay, because the child was growing more shocked and distressed by the minute.

He was taken up within a very short while, and Maddie cleared up the room and went to find her next case. She passed Sarian on the way, and paused briefly beside her.

'Phoned the solicitors yet?'

She nodded. 'Yes. They want to see me as soon as possible. They wouldn't say what it's about, but they can meet me tomorrow at twelve-thirty.'

'But it's your wedding day!' Maddie said under her breath.

'I know, but I have to find out what it's about. It won't take long to get there.'

'You'll have to tell me all about it,' Maddie said.

'Of course I will. We'll be back in the afternoon, anyway. Now I have to fly, I'm doing a back-slab plaster.'

Maddie went to collect her next patient, and for the rest of the day didn't have time to think about Sarian and her letter. Then after work, she collected Angel from the ward and took her to Rob's flat to finish the wedding cake.

'Oh, it's lovely!' Angel said, standing back and looking at it when it was finished.

Maddie had to agree. The cake was round, and they'd stuck little rice-paper rosebuds in a cluster just off centre. The sides were wrapped in creamy yellow ribbon to echo some of the rosebuds, and the whole effect was very fresh and simple and pretty.

'Now all we have to do is arrange some flowers in the chapel, and we're ready. Shall we go and do that?'

Angel nodded, and they went down to the flower shop in the reception area and found a little plastic urn with green florist's foam in it, and picked up the flowers Maddie had ordered. Then they took them to the chapel, arranged them in an arching spray and fixed it on a column kept for the purpose.

'There,' Maddie said, standing back. 'Now, I wonder if Annie's thought about a bouquet or anything?'

Daniel appeared behind her. 'I thought I'd get her

a rose,' he said, looking at the flowers in Maddie's arrangement. They were mostly cream, with a few deep red roses that exactly echoed Angel's dress, and some greenery. 'They're lovely—did you do them?'

'With Angel's help,' Maddie admitted.

'We've been decorating—'

'The flat,' Maddie said quickly, shooting Angel a conspiratorial glance.

Angel covered her mouth with her hand and giggled, and Maddie winked at Daniel and pressed her finger to her lips.

He smiled, a little half-smile that told them he'd allow them their secret, and kissed Maddie on the cheek. 'You're a darling. Right, I'm going home to find a shirt for tomorrow and iron it. I'd better not turn up in crumpled polycotton, or Sarian will change her mind.'

'I somehow doubt it,' Maddie said drily, and he laughed.

'So do I. I'll see you tomorrow—eight-thirty at Rob's? I'm sorry it's so early but it's the only time the chaplain could do, and as it's turned out it's just as well with this meeting at twelve thirty. I'd love to know what it's about.'

'You'll have to possess your soul in patience. I'm just glad she's got you with her. It's not something I'd want her to face alone, whatever they want. I think she finds it all very upsetting still.'

He nodded. 'I'll buy that,' he said, and Maddie wondered for the hundredth time exactly what had happened in his childhood.

Not that it mattered. He and Annie seemed set to move on together, and she was delighted for them both.

If only it didn't highlight *quite* so brightly just how empty her own life was...

It was a beautiful wedding. Sarian looked radiant in her elegant cream dress, her slender figure set off to perfection by the simple cut and clever styling, and behind her stood Angel, her beautiful red dress glowing in the mellow light.

She had flowers in her hair, little simple freesias that stood out against the rich shine of her dark hair, and in the soft lighting of the chapel the fine marks of her surgery hardly showed at all.

She stood proudly behind the bride and groom, carrying the single red rose Daniel had given Sarian. She was holding it as carefully as if it were the secret of eternal life, and Maddie thought the little girl was going to burst with pride and happiness.

The ceremony was very simple and very moving, made all the more so by the sincerity of their vows, and Maddie had to bite her lips hard to prevent herself from crying. It didn't stop the tears from forming and glittering on her lashes, and she hoped no one would notice.

Then Rob reached out a hand and took hers, giving it a reassuring squeeze, and she threw him a slightly embarrassed but grateful smile.

'I always cry at weddings,' she told him a few minutes later while they waited for Daniel and Sarian to sign the register.

'Shall I tell you a secret? I was darned close to it myself,' he confessed in an undertone, and they shared an understanding smile.

They signed as witnesses, then Sarian turned to them with a slightly lost look.

'That's that, then. We're married,' she said, as if she didn't quite know what was supposed to happen next.

'Congratulations,' Maddie said unsteadily, hugging them both in turn, and then Daniel looked at his watch.

'Breakfast somewhere?' he said, looking at the others for confirmation.

'Can we just call in at my flat?' Rob said innocently, but they must have smelled a rat because Daniel and Sarian exchanged an 'Oh, my, what have they done?' glance that made Maddie chuckle.

She pulled out her camera. 'Before we go, we must just have a couple of photos.'

'Let me,' the chaplain said, taking the camera from her and shooing her into line with the others.

He took several of them in various groupings, and then Maddie took one of him with Daniel and Sarian, and then they headed off for Rob's flat, Sarian looking puzzled.

At the top of the stairs Angel could stay silent no longer. 'We've made a secret,' she told them, bursting with excitement and dancing from foot to foot.

'Apparently,' Daniel said drily. 'I thought we weren't having any fuss?'

Maddie clucked. 'Just a little fuss. It *is* your wedding day.'

Rob ushered them in, and then disappeared to the kitchen. 'What's he doing?' Sarian asked, but then he reappeared with a bottle of champagne, beaded with cold from the fridge in the kitchen, and a small tray of canapés he'd bought from a supermarket, and Maddie whisked the cake out of the cupboard and produced some glasses.

'Oh, you shouldn't!' they exclaimed, and there were hugs all round.

'Oh, Maddie, you made a cake,' Sarian said with tears in her eyes.

'I had to. I couldn't let you get married without a wedding cake, Annie—and at least it's not smothered in silver horseshoes and little slippers!'

'I helped her,' Angel said proudly, and showed them how the flowers stuck on.

Daniel, almost speechless with emotion, picked her up and hugged her, and she snuggled into his neck and hugged him back. 'She's really nice,' she said in a stage whisper. 'She looks really pretty.'

'And so do you,' Daniel said warmly, leaning back and looking at her lovingly. 'You look gorgeous, and you were the best bridesmaid ever.'

Angel blushed and giggled, and he set her down, hugged Sarian and took the glass of champagne Rob handed him.

'I'm not making a speech,' Rob said, 'but I'm sure Maddie would join me in wanting to wish you both every happiness in the future. I hope you'll be granted everything you'd wish for yourselves. You deserve it.'

'Hear, hear,' Maddie said, blinking back another rush of tears, and then Angel lifted her tiny glass of champagne and sneezed.

'It went up my nose!' she said with a giggle, and they all laughed, easing the emotional moment.

The cake was delicious, if a little heavy on the brandy, and there was plenty left.

'To send to any friends you want to tell, and for the rest of the department. I thought they'd kill you if you didn't remember them,' Maddie said with a smile.

'You're such a darling,' Sarian said, hugging her again, and out of the corner of her eye Maddie saw Daniel look at his watch.

'I think you two need to make a move if you're going to get to your meeting,' she said. 'Don't forget to tell us all about it.'

'We'll see you later, anyway,' Daniel said. 'We're coming back to the flat this evening.'

'Ah—tonight—Maddie and I thought you might appreciate a little pampering,' Rob said, pulling an envelope out of his jacket and handing it to them.

'What is it?' Daniel said, looking at the envelope suspiciously.

'Open it,' Sarian prompted impatiently, and he did, pulling out a card.

'It's a hotel reservation,' he said, sounding stunned. 'You're sending us away.'

'Only for one night. We can't spare you longer than that,' Maddie said firmly.

'Yes, don't get too used to it.'

'Heavens, have you seen where it is?' Sarian squeaked, reading the card. 'Oh, you are so naughty! Thank you!'

There was another flurry of hugs, and then Daniel ushered her away, leaving them standing around in a lost silence.

'Well, that's that,' Maddie said numbly.

'What happens now?' Angel asked, her face registering disappointment. 'Is it all over? Isn't there a party?'

'That was it,' Rob said.

'Oh.'

She looked so disillusioned that Maddie couldn't ignore it. 'You could come to my parents for lunch tomorrow,' she suggested. 'There will be lots of children there, and it usually turns into a kind of party. If you want to, that is,' she added, belatedly remembering that he was going to be forced to endure her company that evening at the ball as it was. Perhaps he didn't want to see that much of her—

'That would be lovely—if you're sure?' he said, a wistful look in his eyes. 'We haven't shared a big family meal since—well, for ages.'

'Can we, Daddy?' Angel asked, bouncing up and down. 'Please?'

Maddie waited, and he nodded and sent Angel into squeaks of delight.

'And in the meantime,' he put in, 'we might as well finish the canapés.' Rob picked up the plate and passed it to Maddie and Angel. 'Eat up, girls. They won't keep.'

It was a funny old day. Maddie spent the rest of it cleaning her flat and changing her sheets and catching up on her washing. Rob had said he'd pick her up at eight for the ball, and the day seemed interminable.

As she bathed, she wondered for the hundredth time how Annie had got on at the solicitors', but, despite all their promises there was no word from them, and she didn't imagine for a moment they'd bother to come to the ball. Better things to do, she thought with a bittersweet smile, and chided herself for being envious of her friend's happiness.

'It couldn't have happened to a nicer person,' she reminded herself, and stood up, reaching for her towel. If only Rob hadn't been press-ganged, she might feel a bit more enthusiastic about tonight, but she couldn't help wondering if he was only taking her out of duty.

Still, it would be nice to go out, and it was a charity do after all, and usually good fun. She could do with cheering up. She was more concerned about inflicting her parents on him tomorrow, and just hoped they didn't get the wrong end of the stick and start violently matchmaking. That would be too embarrassing for words!

The doorbell rang at a minute to eight, when she was standing in front of the mirror wishing she'd taken Annie's advice and bought another dress. The green was lovely and did wonderful things to her eyes, but, because she'd worn it before, it didn't seem quite special enough, and suddenly she felt as if there was too much flesh on display.

'It's too late for maidenly modesty,' she chided herself, and yanked open the door without giving herself time to fret any more.

He looked gorgeous.

He'd looked smart that morning for the wedding, but like this—well. No wonder it was such a cliché, she thought. Men truly did look superb in dinner suits—and Rob was no exception. The stark white of the dress shirt against the warmth of his skin and the severe black of the jacket was stunning, and he looked taller, straighter—more serious.

Too serious.

She realised she was frowning at him, and gave an embarrassed laugh and held the door open. 'Sorry. You look so different. I was just admiring you.'

A faint wash of colour brushed his neck, and he gave a diffident smile. 'I thought I'd done something wrong,' he said, sounding relieved, then his eyes softened. 'Maddie, you look lovely,' he murmured, and his eyes trailed over every inch of bare skin and made it tingle as if he'd caressed it with a lover's hand.

You're going mad, she thought, and grabbed her jacket and bag. 'All set?' she said.

He nodded. 'I've got a taxi outside. Heard from the others?' he added as he ushered her out.

'No—I was hoping you had. I don't suppose they'll come to the ball.'

'No. Oh, well. They can tell us tomorrow.'

He shut the door of the taxi and they were swept off into the evening traffic. They arrived at the hotel and were carried up the marble steps and towards the ballroom in a tide of partygoers, all glittering and ready for a really good night. The music was playing already, and she could hear the loud buzz of party conversation as they approached the ballroom.

Minutes later they'd shed their coats, found their table with other members of the A and E department, and were drawn into the jollity.

And it was fun, Maddie realised. Rob was entertaining and amusing, and yet he was attentive to her needs, listened to her with every appearance of interest and generally made her feel special.

How kind of him, she thought, and then the MC announced that dinner was served and he stood up. 'Shall we go and start queuing?' he suggested, and she agreed, suddenly realising she hadn't eaten since the wedding breakfast quite early that morning.

'I'm ravenous,' she confessed, and he grinned.

'Good. I hate women that tinker with their food.'

'I never tinker. Food's much too serious,' she said, and they laughed together.

They were still laughing when she turned and saw Sarian approaching, Daniel close behind her.

'Annie!' she said, delighted to see her friend. She had that inner glow, Maddie thought, that came from being well loved—and so did Daniel. Unless she was much mistaken they'd just partaken of the facilities of the honeymoon suite—

'Hey, Easy,' Rob was saying, 'I wasn't expecting to see you here. Changed your mind?' He had a teasing grin on his face, and Maddie thought he'd seen and recognised the same glow she'd noticed.

'Not at all,' Daniel said, and explained they'd wanted to tell them about the meeting.

'What was it all about, Annie?' Maddie asked, unable to restrain her concern a moment longer.

'Their will,' Sarian said. 'Apparently they changed it after I went to visit them that last time, and Mum had written a letter that never got posted...'

Maddie moved closer, offering silent support. 'A letter?' she asked.

And Sarian explained that the letter was an apology for not being more welcoming, but they'd been shocked to see her. Not surprisingly, Maddie thought, considering how their ugly duckling had turned into a beautiful swan. And the revised will directed that all assets except personal ones were to be disposed of and the proceeds given to Sarian to do with as she saw fit.

They would buy a house and give computers to Lizzie's for the patients, and some SIDS monitors for babies at risk of cot death.

'There'll even be enough to buy a better brand of coffee for the staff room,' Daniel teased, 'and some packets of chocolate biscuits.'

'So this really is the end of an era,' Maddie said. 'After your wedding today—'

'Shh,' Daniel warned, but she'd blown it. The words flew round the room, and seconds later someone had told Tim Robertson, the retiring A and E consultant, and Daniel and Sarian found themselves at the front of the ballroom while the band played a fanfare.

'Oops,' Maddie said to Rob, but he grinned.

'High time everyone knew. You can't keep it a secret, and it's not as if they've done anything to be ashamed of!'

Tim was calling everyone to order, and after announcing that they'd been married that morning, he raised his glass, and everyone followed suit.

'To Daniel and Sarian,' he said, and the room echoed with the toast.

'I'll get you for that,' Daniel said with a wry smile, as they stepped off the podium a moment later to cheers and applause.

Maddie smiled apologetically. 'Sorry.'

'Actually, it's nice. Everyone's being lovely,' Sarian said.

'Don't get too involved,' Daniel warned, but it was too late. They were swept away by a crowd of well-wishers, and Maddie was left alone with Rob again.

'I wonder if Peggie and Gareth will turn up after their wedding today?' she mused.

Rob shook his head. 'No. They've had a big family party with lots of her family over from Ireland, I gather, and they're going back there in a day or so to visit the rest during their honeymoon. Did you know his mother's very badly scarred after being burned? She hardly goes out, apparently, and this wedding's a really big thing for her, but Peggie's family adore her and she's making plans to visit them next spring.'

'Oh, how lovely,' Maddie said softly. Peggie was such a little dynamo, and the kindest, sweetest person. If her family were like her, it was no wonder Gareth's mother had been taken to their bosom.

The hullabaloo of the wedding announcement seemed to have died away, and the dance music had struck up again.

'We were queuing for food,' Rob reminded her.

'Yes. We'd better go and get back in the fray.'

It was a delicious buffet, but all of a sudden Maddie found her appetite deserting her, because it had belatedly occurred to her that she was probably going to have to dance with Rob in a moment, and she was afraid she'd give away rather too much in such an intimate embrace.

Perhaps they'd only dance to the faster numbers, she thought wildly, and fiddled with her food, putting off the evil moment.

Then, suddenly, Rob reached over and took her fork out of her hand and stood up. 'It's my favourite song,' he said quietly. 'Dance with me?'

It was a slow song, she realised. Slow and lazy and romantic, and there was no way she could stay out of his arms. Anyway, she didn't want to.

She let him lead her to the dance floor, and as his arms closed around her she gave up the unequal struggle, rested her head on his shoulder and let herself enjoy the luxury of his nearness.

They fitted together perfectly, she thought in a daze. His shoulder was just the right height for her hand to rest on, and her head fitted exactly in the hollow of his shoulder, and his hand against the small of her back exerted just the right amount of pressure—not too much, so that she felt overwhelmed, but enough to guide her as they moved gently together.

His legs brushed hers, his thighs firm and muscled and tantalising, and under her ear she could hear the steady beat of his heart.

The song ended, giving way to another, equally slow and romantic, and she shifted closer, closing the tiny gap so that their bodies chafed against each other with the movement.

Did she imagine it, or was that a low groan that rumbled in his chest? She eased away, but he eased her back again, turning his head so that his lips were close to her ear. She could feel the warm pressure of his jaw against her temple, his lips nuzzling gently at the tip of her ear.

It was comparatively innocent yet unbelievably sensual, and a tiny whimper of need forced its way from her throat.

'Don't,' he groaned, and eased her closer, so that she could feel the solid strength of his body against hers—feel every plane and angle, every last nuance of his desire for her.

He wants me, she thought in stunned amazement.

She lifted her head and met his eyes, and what she saw there made her breath catch in her throat. She stumbled against him and he caught her, making her more aware of him, if that were possible.

'I'm sorry,' he murmured, but she didn't want him to be sorry. Not when she was so glad.

'My fault,' she said, and snuggled against him, not letting him distance them.

They stayed like that till the end, hardly moving, and then the MC wound up the proceedings and they retrieved their coats and headed out into the night. It was cold and crisp and Maddie thought if they walked they might get back some element of common sense, but he hailed a taxi and slotted her into it, and they rode back to her flat in a taut silence only broken by the roar of the traffic and the soft rasp of their breathing.

He paid off the taxi driver, then walked her to the door.

'Thank you for a wonderful evening,' he said gruffly.

'My pleasure. Thank you for taking me. It was lovely.'

She hesitated for the merest second, then made up her mind. If she didn't do this now, she'd go to her grave regretting the wasted opportunity.

'Coffee?' she offered.

He searched her eyes. 'Thank you.'

She fished in her bag for the key, opened the door and led him into her flat, closing the door firmly. Daniel and Sarian were out of the way, nobody else was likely to disturb them. They were alone.

She took off her coat, dropped it over the arm of the sofa and made herself meet his eyes.

'Stay with me,' she said softly, and, in the moment before he closed his eyes, she saw a blazing need so powerful it almost frightened her.

Almost.

He bowed his head forwards, standing silently for several seconds so that she wondered if she'd misread everything and embarrassed him.

Then he lifted his head and looked at her with eyes dark with longing. 'Are you sure?' he said raggedly.

'Yes,' she told him, and realised she was. She was

more sure about this than she'd ever been about anything in her life, and, no matter what the outcome, she would never regret it.

'Yes, I'm sure,' she said firmly, and opened her arms to him.

CHAPTER NINE

MADDIE'S lids fluttered open, and she saw the stormy grey of Rob's eyes just inches away on the pillow. He must have been watching her sleep, and he looked—sad, almost. Her heart stalled for a moment.

'Hi,' she said softly, and his mouth flickered in a slight smile.

'Hi. Are you OK?'

She nodded slightly. 'You?'

'Yes.'

There was an awkward pause, and Maddie thought, oh, no, he regrets it, but then he reached out a hand and brushed a stray lock of hair from her cheek, and his gentle fingers curled around the nape of her neck and drew her towards him.

He met her halfway, his kiss a soft, early-morning caress that told her everything was all right. She sighed and snuggled against him, and he kissed her again, deeper this time, drawing her hard against him so she could feel the heat of his body and the urgency of his desire.

Her own desire spiralled up to meet his, and any worries she might have had about last night's passion being a one-off were blown away by the storm of feeling that rampaged through them, leaving them shaken and boneless.

'Wow,' she said weakly, and he hugged her closer.

'Wow indeed,' he murmured, his breathing still ragged and unsteady. They lay unmoving for a moment, then he kissed her briefly, slid out of bed and disappeared to the bathroom, grabbing his briefs from the floor on the way.

She lay there in the chaos of the bedclothes, filled with a deep contentment and satisfaction she'd never felt before in her life, and wondered where they went from here.

There were the remains of two foil packets on her bedside table, mute testament to their night of passion, and she wondered if he'd anticipated the end of their evening or if he was always prepared, like a good boy scout, just in case.

That left a sour taste in her mouth. Did he do this often? Perhaps it was a regular thing for him, meeting women and striking up a relationship. Nothing permanent, nothing demanding—nothing that smacked of commitment.

She began to feel sick. She loved him. It must be obvious to him by now, although she'd said nothing. At least, she didn't think she had, but he'd made her so mindless with need she might have said anything. And if she had, what did he think?

Because he, certainly, had said nothing to give her any hope.

Then he reappeared, damp from the shower with two mugs in his hands, and she scooted up the bed, dragging the quilt after her and tucking it firmly round her naked breasts.

'I made you tea,' he told her, settling down on the edge of the bed. He was scooping up the bits of foil and crumpling them in his hand, and she thought she'd never get another opportunity.

'It was a good job you had those,' she said, fishing for answers to her unspoken questions.

He opened his palm and looked down at the crumpled foil. 'I always carry some—ever since Maria told me she was pregnant with Angel. That was the only time I've ever been caught without.'

He gave a short, humourless laugh. 'Talk about sod's law. So, yes, I always carry them, and no, I don't use them. I change them every now and then in my wallet, so they're not too old, but I don't use them. In answer to your question, Maria was the last woman I slept with, and that was probably three or four years ago.'

'Three or four years?' Maddie said, horrified. 'But you were married!'

'I told you about our marriage. There was little love lost between us, Maddie, and I don't scratch itches like that. It didn't seem very important compared to what she was doing to Angel.'

He pulled his shirt out of the muddle on the floor and put it on, then tugged on his crumpled trousers.

'I'll iron them,' Maddie offered, but he shook his head.

'Don't bother. I'm going home to change, then I have to see Angel and get her ready for lunch. Are you sure your parents won't mind?'

Heavens, Maddie thought, we're going to lunch! She went to throw back the quilt, but then modesty prevailed and she sank back against the pillows. 'No, they won't mind, but I usually help get things ready. You could follow on later.'

'Or I could come and help,' he offered, filling her with dread. The less time her parents had to interrogate him, the better, but she imagined her mother's antennae would be whirling at the first glance. He was the first man she'd taken home in six years, and she could tell her mother till she was blue in the face that he was a colleague and she'd felt sorry for them because they didn't have anywhere to go and do family things, but her mother wasn't stupid.

Oh, damn.

'You don't need to help,' she protested, but he bent over and gave her a swift kiss.

'No, but I'd like to. Anyway, it will save me getting lost.'

And he stood up, picked up his jacket off the chair in the sitting room and shrugged into it, sticking his head back round the door. 'I'll pick you up later—what time?'

'Eleven-thirty?' she suggested.

He nodded. 'See you later, then.'

She heard the quiet click of the front door, and groaned and rolled over into the pillows. Her mother was going to be all over him like a bloodhound, and her life would be hell!

'Darling! How lovely to see you—and you must be Rob, and this must be Angel. I'm so pleased you could come.'

Maddie's mother bent forwards and hugged her, and smiled welcomingly at Rob and Angel. 'Do come in. The children are in the playroom—they're really looking forward to meeting you, Angel. Maddie, why don't you take her through to meet the others and I'll get Rob a drink?'

Divide and rule, Maddie thought wryly, but she took Angel anyway, holding her hand and leading her through the house to the purpose-built playroom at the back. 'There are lots of children in the family, but

I don't know who's here today,' she told Angel. 'We'll have to see.'

Angel hung back, tugging on her hand. 'I don't want to go in,' she whispered at the door.

Maddie crouched down beside her. 'Don't be shy, love,' she murmured, brushing her hair back off her face. 'They're really nice, and there's lots to do. My mother runs a little club after school, and she's got some really super toys and things.'

'They'll laugh at my face, with all these sticky things on,' she fretted.

Maddie shook her head. 'No, they won't. I'll tell them, if you like, that you've just had an operation and they've got to be very careful with your stitches—I expect they'll be quite impressed, actually. And Sophie's had a bump on the head and spent the night in the hospital recently, so you'll be able to talk to her about what it's like to stay in hospital.'

Angel looked thoughtful, but nodded, and Maddie straightened up and led her through into the room. As usual, it was buzzing with children, and as usual they dropped everything and ran over to hug her.

'Hey, kids, nice to see you,' she said with a laugh, hugging them in turn. Then she put her arm round Angel and hugged her gently. 'This is Angel. She's staying in the hospital at the moment and she's come for lunch with her father. She's just had some stitches in her face, so you have to be careful not to bump her, OK? Sophie, why don't you take Angel and introduce her to everyone, and tell her all about when you were in hospital?'

She stayed a few moments, chatting to some of her nephews and nieces and keeping a surreptitious eye on her little charge. She was settling in well, and so

Maddie went back to the kitchen to find out what her mother had done to Rob.

Nothing too awful, apparently, to her great relief. He was propped up against the worktop, legs crossed at the ankle, a glass of sherry or somesuch cradled in his hand as he laughed at something she was saying. She remembered the way those hands had touched her in the night, and the memory stole her breath.

She hesitated in the doorway, gathering her composure, and he caught sight of her out of the corner of his eye and flashed her a smile which her mother, of course, intercepted.

'Ah, Maddie, darling. You're just in time to make the Yorkshire pudding batter. Rob, why don't you go and find the men and introduce yourself? They're propping up the coffee table in the little sitting room, if I know them. Just down the hall and turn left.'

He winked at Maddie on the way out, and she took a large bowl out of a cupboard and assembled the ingredients. She could hear the cogs turning in her mother's head as she hummed at the stove, and she knew if she waited long enough the questions would start.

Better get in first, she thought.

'He's nice, isn't he?' she said over her shoulder. 'He's working in the same department—he's an old friend of Daniel's, and Angel's in hospital at the moment recovering from plastic surgery, poor little mite. Daniel and Annie got married yesterday, you know. They wouldn't let me tell anyone because they didn't want a lot of fuss, but I've brought you a bit of cake.'

'Annie's married?' her mother said, momentarily distracted.

'Yes—I told you they were engaged last week, but then they decided to get married yesterday.'

'Nice wedding?' she asked.

'Lovely. Very simple. It was just us—and Angel was bridesmaid. That's why I asked them to come here for lunch, because Angel wanted more of a party and I knew the kids would all be here. I hope you don't mind.'

'Of course not.' There was a pause, while she prodded the roast beef and put it back in the oven. 'Rob tells me he took you to the Lizzie's ball last night. Have a good time?'

Maddie closed her eyes and prayed. 'Yes. It was lovely. Daniel and Annie popped in. They looked radiant. I don't think I've ever seen two people so happy.'

'How nice. You look well today,' her mother said, and she wondered if it was in any way connected. Time to change the subject.

'How's Sophie been? You know she came in with her head injury when I was on duty?'

'Yes, of course. She's fine—no repercussions. Right, I think the beef's ready. I'll take it out of the oven to rest. Have you done that batter yet? The pans are nice and hot.'

Maddie handed the bowl of batter over and her mother quickly filled the endless little individual holes in the bun tins and slotted them back into the oven, then turned back to her daughter.

'So how long have you been going out with Rob?' she asked without any pretence at subtlety.

Maddie considered lying, and thought better of it. Her mother wasn't a fool, and she deserved the truth.

'Just last night, really. He's only been at the hospital for two and a half weeks—not even that, quite. I've seen quite a bit of him, of course, because we work together and we've been planning Daniel and Annie's wedding.'

'Quite apart from which, of course, you're in love with him.'

There was no easy answer to that one. She met her mother's eyes over the big kitchen table and gave a wry smile. 'Is it so obvious?'

'Only to me.'

Maddie poured herself a glass of sherry and dropped into a kitchen chair. 'He's widowed,' she told her mother.

'So I gather. He told me about Angel's accident— just briefly, but there's a whole can of worms there, isn't there, that I imagine he didn't really want to open?'

Maddie nodded. 'Maria seems to have gone off the rails towards the end. She told Angel all sorts of things to try and poison her against Rob, and he's tried so hard to be loyal to her and not destroy Angel's memory of her. It's really sad.'

Her mother reached across the table and covered her hand. 'Be careful,' she warned. 'Don't give him the power to hurt you.'

Maddie laughed softly and closed her eyes. 'He already has that.'

'I thought so.' Her mother came round the table and hugged her gently. 'I don't think he'll mean to, and I'm sure it's the last thing he would want, but I just think, if he felt that your relationship with him could adversely affect Angel in any way, he'd end it without hesitation.'

Maddie nodded. 'I'm sure he would. I wouldn't

want anything less. I don't know, Mum. It's all very new—very sudden. Or maybe I've just been very slow to realise what he means to me.'

'Slow? In two weeks?'

She coloured. 'It seems longer.'

'It always does when you're in love. It feels like for ever.' She checked the vegetables, drained them and made the gravy, while Maddie considered the words for ever and longed for what they implied.

She finished her sherry and set the glass down 'I'll go and organise the troops, shall I?' she suggested.

Her mother nodded. 'Please. And, Maddie, be careful. You're very precious. Don't let him make you feel anything less—and remember we're here if you need us.'

'I will. Thanks.' She stood up and dropped a kiss on her mother's cheek, then went off in search of the others. Lunch was nearly ready and it would take time to round up all the children and shuttle them through the cloakroom.

Seating everyone was quite tricky, but they managed it by moving the kitchen table and linking it up with the dining table to make a great long stretch with chairs down both sides. The men did that while the women helped with the lunch and the children, and by the time everything and everyone was ready the Yorkshires were just done and Maddie's father started carving the joint.

Conversation was loud and boisterous and flowed freely, like the wine, and Maddie realised she didn't have to worry about either Rob or Angel. They slotted in as if they'd been there for ever, and her family, in the way of large and boisterous families, made them both entirely welcome.

There would be questions to answer, of course. Brother Tom was looking thoughtful, and she kept intercepting curious glances between her sisters. Oh, well.

'You ought to come for Christmas,' Maddie's mother said after lunch, when they were all sitting round the drawing room fire and sipping tea and coffee. Maddie nearly choked on hers. Whatever had happened to the 'don't let him hurt you' stuff?

'Yes, you should,' her father said. 'Unless, of course, you've got other plans? Madeleine always comes, of course, and this year I think we've got all of them. Accommodation would be a bit tight, but you'd be more than welcome to join us for the day.'

Angel started to bounce up and down. 'Oh, please, Daddy, yes! Can we come? It would be such fun! I really, really want to come.'

He looked at Maddie helplessly, and she shrugged. 'It's up to you. You're more than welcome.'

He turned to her mother. 'May I let you know?'

'Of course. Or just turn up. When you're catering for so many, two more don't make a great deal of difference, and we often get the odd one or two tagging along. Just do whatever you think.'

Maddie wondered if her mother had lost her mind. All that talk about being hurt and Angel having to come first, and now she was matchmaking!

Although, looking at it from her point of view, she probably thought that making him feel welcome would help to cement the bond between him and Maddie. She just hoped it didn't send him screaming!

The conversation moved on, and the next thing was they were talking about accommodation.

'I just want something for a year—a small family

house or a flat or something where Angel can play in the garden, reasonably near a good school and the hospital, and with room for an au pair or something.'

Here again, her family had an opinion and suggestions that would throw them closer together.

'There's a house to let just round the corner, a couple of streets away,' her brother Tom was saying. 'It's a very pleasant little house, three bedrooms or something like that, and off-road parking. The tenants are moving out because they've split up and the landlord's looking for someone now. I could ring him if you like—he's a friend,' Tom explained.

'What about schools and so on?' Rob asked.

'Oh, there's a nice little primary at the end of the road, and of course we run an after-school club,' Maddie's mother told him. 'It would be quite convenient—I could pick her up with the others. Sophie's there, and Andrea's boys. It would be very easy then. You could work as long as you were needed, and you could always get a babysitter for the nights you're on call.'

Maddie was amazed. Talk about working fast! She tried to warn her mother off, but she was oblivious.

Finally she managed to drag Rob out before her father called the vicar to marry them, and on the way back they detoured and looked at the outside of the house Tom had mentioned. It looked like a pleasant little house as Tom had said, nothing special, but affordable and pretty and above all convenient.

'Looks good,' Rob said thoughtfully. 'I'll have to go round and see it. Are you sure your mother wouldn't mind having Angel? It would be a perfect solution, as she got on so well with the others.'

Maddie all but rolled her eyes. 'I'm sure she wouldn't mind,' she said. 'In fact, she'd be delighted.'

They went back to Maddie's flat and dropped her off, and Rob left Angel in the car and walked her to the door. 'Thanks, Maddie,' he said softly. 'For last night and today. It's been—' He shook his head, as if he was lost for words, and then bent forwards and pressed a quick, hard kiss on her lips. 'I'll ring you,' he murmured, then turned on his heel and strode swiftly down the path.

She heard the car door shut, then the revs pick up as he pulled away.

So he was possibly going to be living a few streets from her parents, with Angel in the after-school club and at the same school as some of her nephews and nieces.

And what would happen then if he decided Maddie wasn't a good influence?

It was all getting too complicated too fast, and Maddie felt that the cart was definitely being put before the horse. Either that, or he didn't consider their relationship so significant that it was worth worrying about.

Even though she was the first woman he'd made love to in three or four years?

Maybe she was the first one he'd had time to cultivate. After all, he'd taken Maria up on her offer without hesitation.

Oh, damn. She let herself into the flat, changed the sheets on the bed and stuffed them in the washing machine downstairs, and was just coming back up when Daniel and Sarian came down the stairs with their arms round each other.

'You're here at last!' they said, smiling cheerfully, and Maddie felt assailed by loneliness.

'Yes—we went to my parents for lunch.'

'We?' Sarian said.

'Angel wanted more of a party after the wedding, and it's always a party at my parents'. So, how was the hotel?'

They coloured slightly in unison.

'Wonderful,' Sarian said softly. 'Thank you so much. It was utter luxury. We had breakfast in bed—champagne and orange juice and all sorts of lovely pastries. It was the most disgusting indulgence—I'm sure I've put on stones.'

'We did go for a walk afterwards to work it off,' Daniel reminded her, and she grinned.

'Only a short walk. Is the kettle on?'

Maddie nodded. 'It's always on. Come on in.'

Daniel dropped into a chair and turned on the television, and Sarian followed Maddie to the kitchen.

'So, tell me all about the ball,' she demanded, plopping herself down at the table and staring at Maddie expectantly. 'You and Rob seemed to be getting on rather well.'

Maddie felt hot colour crawl up her cheeks, and busied herself with mugs and tea bags and the kettle, which needed absolutely no attention whatsoever. 'He was a very attentive partner,' she said calmly.

'Attentive, eh? Tell me more!'

The colour deepened, and suddenly the uncertainty of her feelings boiled over. 'Annie, butt out,' she said bluntly. 'I'm not quizzing you about your wedding night, and I don't expect you to ask me questions about what Rob and I got up to.'

There was a shocked silence, then Sarian apologised stiffly. Maddie dropped her head forwards, biting her lip to stop the tears.

'It's all right. It's just—I don't know how he feels.'

She heard the scrape of a chair, and her friend's arms came round her from behind and hugged her gently. 'It's hell, isn't it? Give him time. From what Daniel's said Maria was a bitch. He's not got very good memories of marriage, so I don't suppose he's in a hurry to get back in there, and he's got Angel to consider. Maybe he just needs time to get used to the idea.'

'And maybe he isn't even that interested,' Maddie said flatly. 'Whatever. Here, the kettle's boiled.'

Sarian released her and she made the tea, handed her two mugs and picked up the other one and a packet of biscuits. 'Let's go and feed your man. No doubt you've worn him out.'

Apparently she had. Daniel was asleep, snoring softly in front of the television, and Sarian prodded him and gave him his tea. He yawned and stretched, threw Maddie a lazy grin and reached for a biscuit.

'Cheers, Maddie,' he said, and she wondered why she'd worried about losing his company. It seemed she'd gained them both!

Still, it was better than sitting around on her own and moping.

They left after an hour, though, and it was after nine before Rob rang.

'Hi,' he said softly. 'I'm sorry I've been so long. I had to settle Angel and she was really excited—she seems to have enjoyed the day.' He paused, then went on, 'I don't suppose you want to come round and share a take-away? I'll pick you up.'

She laughed. 'I couldn't eat a thing!' she confessed.

'Oh. Well, don't worry, then,' Rob said, and he sounded disappointed.

'No—Rob, wait!' she said hastily. 'I don't want to eat, but I'd love to come round. I can watch you eat, I don't mind.'

He laughed softly. 'I'm not hungry either. I just wanted an excuse to see you again. Stay there, I'll pick you up in five minutes.'

'I can't—'

He'd put the phone down, and Maddie rolled her eyes and studied herself in the mirror in despair. She needed to put her face on, tidy her hair, change—

'Why?' she asked herself. 'He fancied you this morning with last night's mascara running down your cheeks. Don't fuss.'

She brushed her hair, cleaned her teeth and changed into something soft and comfy—something suitable for curling up next to him in front of the television.

Then she went outside, just as his car pulled up, and slid in beside him. He leant over and gave her a kiss, harmless enough, but it set her pulse racing.

It was a waste of time doing her hair, changing her clothes, putting on the lipstick. He closed the door of his flat behind them, pulled her into his arms and kissed her as if he was dying for her. Finally he came up for air and smiled a lopsided, ragged little smile.

'I need you,' he confessed unsteadily.

'I need you, too.'

All the humour drained from his face, replaced by a hunger that should have frightened her. His hands cupped her cheeks, trembling slightly, and he kissed her again, slowly this time, fuelling the fire.

This time when he lifted his head it was to scoop

her into his arms and carry her to the bed. He dropped her into the middle of it, stripped off his clothes and reached for her, peeling the sweater over her head and tugging the soft-knit skirt down over her hips.

Her underwear vanished in seconds, and then he was there, his body hard against her, plundering her mouth with his while his hands did incredible things to her. Then he rolled away, and she heard the tearing sound of foil.

'Damn, my hands are shaking so much I can't do this!' he muttered, and she knelt up beside him and helped him.

She wasn't sure if it made it better or worse, but they tumbled laughing back into the bed and he drew her up against him and kissed her again. 'Oh, Maddie,' he said softly, and then he moved over her, his powerful body surging into her, completing her.

I love you, she thought, and closed her eyes against the threatening tears. Please, God, don't let him be using me. Let it be real. Let it be for ever...

CHAPTER TEN

MADDIE felt like death warmed up. She'd had very little sleep on Saturday night, last night she'd been with Rob until he'd taken her home at three, and she'd been up at six-thirty because, joy of joys, she was on an early.

And to crown it all, when she went into work the first person she saw was young Ben, the skateboarder, being brought in on a stretcher. He was shifting restlessly, and even as she walked towards him Maddie could hear him struggling for breath.

'Hello, Ben,' she said, resting her hand on his arm. 'What's happened?' she asked the ambulanceman.

'His mum just went to wake him up and he's hardly conscious. Chest injury. She said something about breaking his ribs a couple of weeks ago?' he told her. 'I'm not a paramedic but I think he's got a tension pneumothorax.'

It certainly looked like it. Maddie scanned him quickly, noting the signs, and then miraculously Rob appeared at her side. 'Problems?'

'Yes—Ben. Query tension pneumothorax. His breathing's laboured, his pulse is weak and rapid, his jugular veins are distended—that's just a first glance.'

'Good girl. Right, let's get him into X-ray and find out what's going on.'

'I just found him like this this morning,' Ben's mother told them. 'He was out with his friends last night—he said he wasn't going to take the board, but

I suppose he must have done. He came back in at nine, stuck his head round the door and said he was going to bed, and I didn't see him again until this morning. Then—'

She shrugged helplessly, and Rob rested a hand on her shoulder briefly. 'Don't worry. We'll find out what's going on. I suspect he's fallen on those ribs and pushed them in a bit or something. Just take a seat and we'll get some pictures. Right, Ben, let's find out what you've done.'

The X-rays, however, showed more than they wanted to see. 'He's got a definite pneumothorax,' Rob murmured, looking at the large black area of air inside his chest. 'Those ribs are a mess now. One of them's snapped clean through and one end has penetrated the pleural cavity and nicked his lung.'

'He must have been in agony! Why didn't he tell his mother?' Maddie said, stunned.

'Because he's a bloody fool and he knew he'd get a hiding,' Rob retorted. 'We need to get him up to theatre and get those ribs out of the way, but we need to deal with the pneumothorax first. Maddie, can you call the orthopaedic team? I'll talk to Mum.'

She paged the doctor on call, then went with Rob into Resus. He worked fast, and by the time the orthopaedic reg turned up a few moments later Ben's chest was decompressing and he was much better. His breathing was improving, his neck veins were going down and his life was no longer under threat.

The surgeon looked at the X-rays, agreeing that he needed immediate surgery.

'I'll go and get ready. Can you send him up? I think we might put him in a body cast this time till he's healed.'

Maddie smiled, and Ben's mother, lurking anxiously on the other side of the room, gave a slightly hysterical laugh. 'What a good idea,' she said. 'Alternatively I'll just shoot him, shall I?'

'Oh, no, please don't. It's Monday morning. It'll make such a mess!'

They laughed, releasing the tension, and Maddie patted Ben on the shoulder. 'All right, old chap? Feeling better now?'

He nodded weakly. 'Thanks. Sorry.'

'Don't apologise to me, petal. It's your mum you need to apologise to. She's aged about ten years since I last saw her.'

Ben left the department a few minutes later, and Maddie turned to Rob with a smile. 'What are you doing here so early?' she asked softly. 'Not that I'm not pleased to see you, with a crisis like that and a tired junior doctor who's been on call all weekend.'

He grinned. 'I couldn't stay away,' he said teasingly, and Maddie wondered how true it was. Probably very true, to get him out of bed after only three hours' sleep.

It gave her a warm feeling inside.

She was just going off duty at three when Rob cornered her by the lockers and dropped a swift kiss on her lips. 'I've spoken to your brother—he rang about the house, and I've had a word with the landlord and I'm looking at it tonight. Want to come?'

She nodded. 'Love to. What time?'

'Seven, I have to be there. Pick you up at six-thirty?'

She nodded again. 'Fine. I'm going back to bed now,' she said with a grin. 'Catch up a bit.'

'Get some for me,' he chuckled, and with a wink he left her and went back to his patients.

Maddie went home, fished the sheets out of the tumble drier where she'd put them that morning and made her bed, then fell into it. She'd had to sleep on the bed without sheets last night, because by the time she'd come home after three, she'd been too tired to worry.

She was woken by the doorbell at six-thirty, and leapt out of bed, dragged on the clothes she'd worn briefly the night before and scraped a brush through her hair before opening the door.

'Sorry, I was still asleep,' she said with an apologetic smile. 'Come in for a moment.'

'I've got Angel in the car. I'll wait out here,' he told her, and gave her a quick kiss.

He was doing that a lot, she realised as she found her shoes and grabbed her bag and coat. Was it significant? He'd seemed so self-contained at first. Was this the real Rob?

Whatever, she was enjoying it. She slammed the door of the flat, ran out and slid into the car beside him, throwing Angel a smile in the back. 'Hi, love. How are you?'

'OK—we're going to see our new house,' Angel told her. 'I'm going to be out of hospital soon, and we need a bigger house than Daddy's flat, 'cos it's too small for both of us, so we're having this one.'

'Well, we might,' Rob cautioned. 'We might not like it.'

But they did. It was lovely—the garden was apparently west-facing, the rooms had big windows and would be bright and sunny, and it was in a good state of repair. It was unfurnished, but Rob had a house full of furniture in store, he said.

'I don't suppose there's any chance I could be in by Christmas, is there?' he asked the landlord.

'Sure. It's empty now—you can have it as soon as the lease is drawn up. Friday?'

'Excellent. I'll have to arrange to have the furniture delivered.'

Angel started bouncing. 'We're going to have a house again,' she chirruped, and ran back upstairs to look at 'her' room.

Maddie went to retrieve her, casting a longing look at the master bedroom which overlooked the pretty garden. Would she ever be in there with Rob? Or would their time together come to an end once Angel was out of hospital?

She'd healed so well that the only thing keeping her there really was their accommodation problem. And now it was solved, their opportunities to be alone were going to be severely restricted.

'What will you do with Angel during the Christmas holidays?' she asked him later that evening after Angel was back on the ward.

He sighed. 'I don't know. The hospital run a crèche, but I think she would probably be insulted if I suggested it. Got any ideas?'

She did, but she thought she was mad to mention it. 'My parents run a holiday club,' she told him. 'They took early retirement from a prep school that they owned in Hertfordshire, and set themselves up here so they could enjoy their grandchildren. Just by coincidence we're all in a ten mile radius, and as they seemed to be looking after them all the time, they decided to make it a business.'

'Some retirement,' Rob said wryly.

'They love it. They'd be lost without the children. Anyway, I'm sure Angel would be welcome to join them for the holidays, and she could always spend the day on the ward occasionally if they were busy or closed.'

Rob nodded. 'And I'll have to find a babysitter for the nights I'm on call. I ought to advertise, I suppose.'

'Mum will know someone,' she told him.

And that was that organised, she thought. Another thread binding him to her.

But what if it all went wrong? What if their relationship foundered?

Not that it mattered. She didn't live with her parents, but she had to work with him all day anyway. It couldn't be much more awkward than that.

She'd just have to hope it didn't happen.

Christmas was less than a week away, and already it was snowing. On the Thursday night, the night before Rob's furniture was being delivered, they had snow so deep it came up over Maddie's ankles. She set off for work in boots, trudging through the snow on a bright, sparkling morning that made her heart feel lighter.

Not that it was the sun that was up! Oh, no. At something past six in late December, it was the street lights that were shining, gleaming on the snow with an eerie yellow sheen like something out of a movie.

It was strangely silent, as well, the noise of traffic muted by the muffling blanket of snow that enveloped everything. It hung on the trees, huge piles of it that later would melt and plop to the ground, but now it was fine and powdery and fell like dust if she touched a branch.

The sky was lightening as she arrived at work, and she stamped her feet and shook the snow from her coat before going in and changing into her shoes and tabard.

'Gorgeous morning,' she said to Charity.

The nurse looked at her as if she were crazy. 'Maddie, it's *snowing!* How can it be gorgeous?'

'I love it. Makes it seem like Christmas.' She tugged her tabard straight and pinned her watch to it. 'How's the boyfriend?'

Charity's face softened, and her eyes lit up. 'Wonderful. He's so nice. He's taking me to meet his mother at Christmas.'

'Wow—serious stuff!' Maddie said, forgetting that Rob and Angel were spending Christmas with her and her parents. 'Oh, Charity, I do hope it works out.'

She smiled, the contented smile of a woman in love, and Maddie wondered if her own smile was as transparent, because for all Rob's affectionate kisses and their stolen hours together, there was still no talk of love between them.

Maybe he was just being cautious. Or maybe it was even worse than that.

She hurried about her work, trying to blank her mind to the terrifying possibility that he was just using her because of her parents' crèche facilities.

It wouldn't be the first time she'd misread a man's intentions, after all.

The house was wonderful. Angel spent the entire weekend rediscovering all her possessions, and Rob was busy doing the same. It was the books he'd missed, all the reference books and art books and the 'keepers', those novels that didn't get chucked in a bag for a jumble sale but stayed, to be read and enjoyed again and again.

When he'd packed up the house after Maria's death, and cleared away all the personal things that reminded him too much of the bitter struggle their marriage had been, he'd felt lighter.

Now, unpacking what remained, he felt almost as if he'd got his life back again. He had a house, albeit temporary, he had Angel almost back to normal, both in body and spirit—and he had Maddie.

How long for, he didn't know. The thought of marriage terrified him, but the thought of being without her was possibly even worse.

Angel bounced into the room with an ancient teddy, and threw herself into his arms. 'It's really nice here, Daddy,' she said, burrowing into his shoulder. 'I'm so glad I'm living with you again. I've missed you.'

'I've missed you, too, poppet,' he said, choked, and forgot about the future. The present was too good to squander on idle speculation, and time would take care of everything. For now, he was just going to enjoy his daughter.

She spent Saturday back on the ward, because he was on duty, and it was a harrowing day. He lost a child, a little girl the same age as Angel, just two days before Christmas. He sat with the parents, going over the reasons why she'd died, explaining about the pneumonia and how sometimes a bug could attack so fast and so hard that nothing could be done, and he wondered if she had presents under the tree and how they would survive all the Christmases to follow.

And when they'd gone he ran up to the ward, found Angel in the playroom and gave her a hug. 'All right, my pretty little Angel?' he asked, his voice still shaky.

'Yeah, fine. I'm making Christmas decorations for our tree.' She tipped her head up and gave him a searching look. 'Aren't you supposed to be at work?'

He nodded, swallowing hard. 'Yes. I'm going back now. I just wanted to say hi. I'll see you later.'

'OK.' She stretched up and kissed him, and he squeezed her shoulder and went back down to A and E. It was crazy, but he'd just had to see her, to assure himself that she was still alive. She'd come so close—

Too close. He threw himself back into work, and that night he unpacked the Christmas decorations and he and Angel put the tree up and hung it with her little paper tree ornaments that she'd made on the ward, and in the morning they sat down and watched a film together.

He rang Maddie that evening and talked to her about the arrangements for Christmas Day, and she told him to make his way over there for twelve o'clock. Then he took Angel for a drive and they looked at the Christmas lights, and then he put her to bed and thought about the parents of the little girl he'd lost the day before, and wondered if Angel missed her mother or if her memory was now just a distant blur.

Then he thought of Maddie, of her warmth and softness and generous touch, and his body ached to hold her.

Sleep was a long time coming.

It was a white Christmas. Maddie had spent the evening wrapping presents, and in the morning she loaded them all up into her little car which she'd kept overnight at the flat especially for this, and slithered off the drive. The roads had been cleared, and she arrived safely at her parents' house in time to distribute the presents to all and sundry.

There were just two left—a house-warming present for Rob of a rug for the hall, and a game for Angel. Nothing inspired, nothing that could be taken out of context—nothing to provoke comment.

He arrived laden with wine and chocolates and a plant for her mother, and Angel was greeted with cries of delight by the others, who rushed to show her their presents.

Lunch was chaotic, as ever, with balloons and streamers and crackers and silly hats, and Rob joined in with a slightly bemused look on his face.

Angel was delicious in her lovely red dress, and much admired, and for the first time she didn't have to have the Steri-Strips on to hold her incisions.

'She looks lovely,' Maddie's mother said softly, following the direction of Maddie's gaze.

'She is. She's still got a bit of a limp, but Rob says they'll sort that out later on if it doesn't resolve. She's having physio and it's getting better, apparently.'

'And how are things with Rob?'

Maddie shrugged. 'Fine. I still have no idea what he feels for me.'

Her mother smiled. 'Don't you? I can tell a mile away.'

'You just see what you want to see,' Maddie told her bluntly, not daring to hope.

'I don't think so.' She swirled her tea thoughtfully in the cup. 'Why don't you let Angel stay here for the night, and go and talk it over with him?'

'What? Say, "Oh, by the way, I love you. I just wondered if it was mutual"? You must be nuts!'

'I didn't perhaps have quite that in mind, but I think you need to know where you stand for everybody's sake. Angel needs security.'

Maddie sighed. 'I know that. I just don't feel I can push him.'

'You mean you don't want to know that he's toying with you,' her mother said sagely.

'Yes. That too. Where is he, anyway?'

'In the study with your father. They've discovered that Rob's father was at school with him, and they're looking up old photos. I'm going to put the kettle on again.'

'I'll do it,' Maddie said, glad to get away. The conversation was a little too close to the bone for her, and her mother was like a terrier. She wondered what they were talking about in the study, and decided she didn't want to know.

'I gather Rob's taken the house,' Tom said, catching her in the kitchen.

'Yes. It's lovely. He's really pleased. Thanks for doing that.'

'My pleasure. He's a nice guy. You could do worse.'

'He's just a colleague, Tom,' she protested, but Tom smiled.

'Whatever you say, sister dear. That's not the way my colleagues look at me, believe me.'

She went upstairs and hid in the bathroom for a minute, perching on the edge of the bath and wondering how long she'd be in peace before someone needed the loo. She loved her family, but today everyone seemed determined to meddle and interfere, in the nicest possible way.

It was going to drive her mad.

'Oops, sorry.'

She opened the door and came out, smiling ruefully at her sister Kate. 'I was hiding.'

'It is a bit much,' she said with a grin, then grabbed Maddie's arm and dropped her voice to a whisper. 'He's gorgeous. Has he popped the question yet?'

Maddie rolled her eyes. 'No. He probably isn't going to.'

'Shame. Oh, well, keep me in touch.'

'I will.' She escaped to the kitchen and immersed herself in washing up water. Moments later Rob appeared beside her, tea towel in hand, and started drying up.

'I've just found out our fathers were at school together,' he told her. 'We've been looking at photos.'

'Mmm. Mum said. Did he remember your father?'

'Vaguely. He was older, of course.' He put the pan down and picked up another. 'It's a shame my father's dead. They could have talked about old times. He was good at that.'

Maddie laughed. 'They always are.' She pulled the last dregs of cutlery out of the sink, handed them to Rob and washed the bubbles from her hands. 'Tea?'

'I'll sink if I have any more tea. What time are we supposed to go?'

Maddie laughed. 'Nobody goes. The children all camp down in the playroom, and the adults all sleep in the bedrooms. The older kids keep an eye on the younger ones, and the party just carries on tomorrow.'

'I have to work tomorrow.'

'So do I. What's Angel doing? She could stay

here—the night as well,' she added, thinking that maybe her mother was right and the suspense was killing her. Anyway, she'd made a decision and she had a proposal to put to him.

Literally.

'That would be good,' he said softly. 'Maybe we could grab some time alone together.'

She looked up at him. 'We could go back to your house.'

He nodded, a slow, sexy smile playing over his lips. 'Yes, we could. I'll go home and get Angel some things, if you think it's all right for her to stay. Should I check with your mother?'

'She suggested it,' Maddie told him. 'I'm sure it's fine.'

'Aiding and abetting?' he murmured.

'Like you wouldn't believe,' Maddie said under her breath as he left the room to ask Angel.

Needless to say his daughter thought it was a brilliant idea, and Rob, bundled up against the cold, went to fetch her night things.

They had tea, a desultory affair consisting of a few sandwiches and a couple of plates of sausage rolls that nobody wanted, followed by Christmas cake that hardly anybody could fit in, and more cups of tea.

'No wonder you're a tea drinker,' Rob said under his breath.

And then finally, at about seven o'clock when Maddie's nerves were strung as tight as a bowstring, she stood up and went over to Rob who was battling with one of the boys on a video game. 'Shall we?'

He nodded, put his joystick down and stood up, unravelling his long legs from the floor. 'You win,' he said to the boy, and bent to kiss Angel. 'You be good, now. I'll see you in the morning.'

She grinned and turned back to her new friends, and they made their farewells and escaped.

'That was a lovely day,' Rob said, throwing his arm around her shoulder.

Maddie, ready to snap, didn't feel like a lazy stroll. She wanted to hurry back to his house and get it over with. 'I'm cold,' she said, not altogether untruthfully. 'Can we walk a bit faster?'

'Of course,' he said, and fell into step beside her. It only took a few minutes to walk to the house, and when they arrived, she took off her coat and hung it on the hook in the cloakroom, then looked at herself. She looked healthy, her skin rosy from the food and exercise, and if her eyes were a little overbright, it didn't really show.

Nor, amazingly, did the tangle of nerves inside her stomach that the butterflies were using as a roller coaster.

She went back to the sitting room, and found Rob lighting the coal-effect gas fire. The lights were turned down, there was soft music playing, and he straightened up as she went in and looked at her searchingly.

'Rob—'

'Maddie—'

They laughed a little tensely, and he gestured to her. 'You go first.'

She took a steadying breath, and forced herself to meet his eyes. 'I love you,' she said without preamble. 'I know you probably don't feel the same, but we seem to get on well enough, and I love Angel so much it hurts. She needs a mother, and you need a wife. If you'll marry me, I'll do everything I can to make you both happy.'

She ground to a halt, running out of words, and he closed his eyes and gave a grunt of laughter.

'Don't laugh at me!' she cried, agonised by his reaction, and he opened his eyes and reached for her.

'I wasn't. Darling, I wasn't. It was just the irony. I wanted to bring you back here to ask you to marry me, and you beat me to it.'

She stared at him in amazement. 'What?' she said blankly.

'I was going to ask you to marry me. I've got my mother's ring in my pocket.' He pulled it out, then took her hand and slipped a lovely, simple diamond ring onto her finger. 'It fits,' he said.

'But—why?' she asked, still unable to believe it.

He laughed softly. 'Because I love you. Because, despite all my fears, the only thing that terrifies me more than marriage is the thought of life without you. Because I love you, Maddie Brooks, and you've brought me and my daughter back to life again and given us hope.'

He cupped her face in his hands and looked down at her with tender eyes. 'I don't think you can have any idea of what you gave me when you asked me to stay the night after the ball. That, and taking me to meet your parents, and their friendly acceptance of us, and of Angel's problems.'

'She's lovely—she's a darling. Of course they love her.'

'And they accepted her just as she is.'

'She's fine.'

'But she wasn't, and I know it wouldn't have been any different. Everyone would have been just the same. And you've been wonderful with her, but that's not why I want to marry you. It's important—it's vital, but it wouldn't make me love you. Only you've done that, with your warmth and your kindness and your silly sense of humour. Marry me, Maddie. Make me whole again.'

'Oh, yes,' she said, throwing herself into his arms and sobbing with happiness. 'Oh, yes, please.'

'Thank God for that,' he said shakily, and hugged her so hard her ribs creaked. 'Oh, Maddie, I love you.'

'I love you, too,' she mumbled into his shirt. 'You're the best thing that's ever happened to me, Robert Oliver, and I'm going to make darned sure that you don't live to regret this.'

'Good. Fancy working on the next generation?'

'What about Angel? Shouldn't we go back and tell her?'

He eased away from her with a rueful smile. 'I suppose so, if you feel you can cope with your family again.'

'Can you?' she asked, worried now that they'd overwhelmed him.

He laughed. 'Of course I can. They're wonderful. And you're right, we ought to tell Angel.'

She smiled. 'There's always later,' she told him.

'I'll hold you to that.'

They put their coats on again and went out, walking hand in hand along the quiet snow-covered streets, and let themselves into the house. Angel was coming out of the playroom as they hung up their coats, and she ran up to them in puzzlement.

'Why have you come back? Can't I stay?'

'Of course you can stay. We've got something to

tell you. I've asked Maddie to marry me, and she's said yes.'

There was a gasp from behind them, and a loud shushing as her family waited in suspense. They didn't have to wait long.

Angel's eyes lit up brighter than the Christmas tree. 'Oh, Daddy! That's brilliant! It's what I asked Father Christmas for, and it's come true! Oh, it's the best Christmas ever!'

And Maddie, hugging and kissing everyone in the midst of popping champagne corks, had to agree. It really had been the very best Christmas ever.

™ MILLS & BOON®

FEBRUARY 2010 HARDBACK TITLES

ROMANCE

At the Boss's Beck and Call	Anna Cleary
Hot-Shot Tycoon, Indecent Proposal	Heidi Rice
Revealed: A Prince and A Pregnancy	Kelly Hunter
Hot Boss, Wicked Nights	Anne Oliver
The Millionaire's Misbehaving Mistress	Kimberly Lang
Between the Italian's Sheets	Natalie Anderson
Naughty Nights in the Millionaire's Mansion	Robyn Grady
Sheikh Boss, Hot Desert Nights	Susan Stephens
Bought: One Damsel in Distress	Lucy King
The Billionaire's Bought Mistress	Annie West
Playboy Boss, Pregnancy of Passion	Kate Hardy
A Night with the Society Playboy	Ally Blake
One Night with the Rebel Billionaire	Trish Wylie
Two Weeks in the Magnate's Bed	Nicola Marsh
Magnate's Mistress…Accidentally Pregnant	Kimberly Lang
Desert Prince, Blackmailed Bride	Kim Lawrence
The Nurse's Baby Miracle	Janice Lynn
Second Lover	Gill Sanderson

HISTORICAL

The Rake and the Heiress	Marguerite Kaye
Wicked Captain, Wayward Wife	Sarah Mallory
The Pirate's Willing Captive	Anne Herries

MEDICAL™

Angel's Christmas	Caroline Anderson
Someone To Trust	Jennifer Taylor
Morrison's Magic	Abigail Gordon
Wedding Bells	Meredith Webber

FEBRUARY 2010 LARGE PRINT TITLES

ROMANCE

Desert Prince, Bride of Innocence — Lynne Graham

Raffaele: Taming His Tempestuous Virgin — Sandra Marton

The Italian Billionaire's Secretary Mistress — Sharon Kendrick

Bride, Bought and Paid For — Helen Bianchin

Betrothed: To the People's Prince — Marion Lennox

The Bridesmaid's Baby — Barbara Hannay

The Greek's Long-Lost Son — Rebecca Winters

His Housekeeper Bride — Melissa James

HISTORICAL

The Brigadier's Daughter — Catherine March

The Wicked Baron — Sarah Mallory

His Runaway Maiden — June Francis

MEDICAL™

Emergency: Wife Lost and Found — Carol Marinelli

A Special Kind of Family — Marion Lennox

Hot-Shot Surgeon, Cinderella Bride — Alison Roberts

A Summer Wedding at Willowmere — Abigail Gordon

Miracle: Twin Babies — Fiona Lowe

The Playboy Doctor Claims His Bride — Janice Lynn

0210 Gen Std HB

MILLS & BOON

MARCH 2010 HARDBACK TITLES

ROMANCE

Greek Tycoon, Inexperienced Mistress	Lynne Graham
The Master's Mistress	Carole Mortimer
The Andreou Marriage Arrangement	Helen Bianchin
Untamed Italian, Blackmailed Innocent	Jacqueline Baird
Bought: Destitute yet Defiant	Sarah Morgan
Wedlocked: Banished Sheikh, Untouched Queen	Carol Marinelli
The Virgin's Secret	Abby Green
The Prince's Royal Concubine	Lynn Raye Harris
Married Again to the Millionaire	Margaret Mayo
Claiming His Wedding Night	Lee Wilkinson
Outback Bachelor	Margaret Way
The Cattleman's Adopted Family	Barbara Hannay
Oh-So-Sensible Secretary	Jessica Hart
Housekeeper's Happy-Ever-After	Fiona Harper
Sheriff Needs a Nanny	Teresa Carpenter
Sheikh in the City	Jackie Braun
The Doctor's Lost-and-Found Bride	Kate Hardy
Desert King, Doctor Daddy	Meredith Webber

HISTORICAL

The Viscount's Unconventional Bride	Mary Nichols
Compromising Miss Milton	Michelle Styles
Forbidden Lady	Anne Herries

MEDICAL™

Miracle: Marriage Reunited	Anne Fraser
A Mother for Matilda	Amy Andrews
The Boss and Nurse Albright	Lynne Marshall
New Surgeon at Ashvale A&E	Joanna Neil

0210 Gen Std LP

MARCH 2010 LARGE PRINT TITLES

ROMANCE

A Bride for His Majesty's Pleasure — Penny Jordan
The Master Player — Emma Darcy
The Infamous Italian's Secret Baby — Carole Mortimer
The Millionaire's Christmas Wife — Helen Brooks
Crowned: The Palace Nanny — Marion Lennox
Christmas Angel for the Billionaire — Liz Fielding
Under the Boss's Mistletoe — Jessica Hart
Jingle-Bell Baby — Linda Goodnight

HISTORICAL

Devilish Lord, Mysterious Miss — Annie Burrows
To Kiss a Count — Amanda McCabe
The Earl and the Governess — Sarah Elliott

MEDICAL™

Secret Sheikh, Secret Baby — Carol Marinelli
Pregnant Midwife: Father Needed — Fiona McArthur
His Baby Bombshell — Jessica Matthews
Found: A Mother for His Son — Dianne Drake
The Playboy Doctor's Surprise Proposal — Anne Fraser
Hired: GP and Wife — Judy Campbell